Thank you for your
support Mike!

Enjoy "In Due Time"

IN DUE TIME

AL JOHNSON

IN DUE TIME

iUniverse books may be ordered through booksellers or by contacting:

iUniverse
1663 Liberty Drive
Bloomington, IN 47403
www.iuniverse.com
844-349-9409

Because of the dynamic nature of the Internet, any web addresses or links contained in this book may have changed since publication and may no longer be valid. The views expressed in this work are solely those of the author and do not necessarily reflect the views of the publisher, and the publisher hereby disclaims any responsibility for them.

Any people depicted in stock imagery provided by Getty Images are models, and such images are being used for illustrative purposes only. Certain stock imagery © Getty Images.

ISBN: 978-1-6632-2023-3 (sc)
ISBN: 978-1-6632-2024-0 (e)

Library of Congress Control Number: 2021906432

Print information available on the last page.

iUniverse rev. date: 04/08/2021

CONTENTS

CHAPTER 1

"Leaving"

AS THE BUS TRAVELED DOWN the inner-city streets of Chicago, the city that Gerald had called home for the past thirty-five years as he took in tear filled glimpses while watching the people walking the streets of the early morning to start their day. The bus made a right-hand turn onto Munson Street passing by the lounge and bar that he met the woman he thought would be his forever one true love, he affectionately called Nina. As the bus passed by the lounge and bar

Mr. Paul was raising the gates to open up for the morning crowd at Centerfield Lounge and Bar. Flashbacks of the many nights he spent there until the bartender Mike would yell out, "last call to play ball" went through his mind. As the sound of the acceleration came from the bus's engine roared through the floor, he thought it would be the last time he would see the famous Chicago "Centerfield Lounge and Bar" at least for a while as Munson Street entered onto Interstate Ninety-Four. All green lights ahead like the future he was praying for down the road in the big city of Atlanta that once included Nina. The tears swelled in his eyes and began to roll down his face but, deep down inside he knew it was best for them both but, more so for him now. There was an older lady seated next to him that leaned over and whispered in Gerald's ear,

"Nobody ever said new beginnings would be so easy young man" as she rubbed his hand and slipped him some of her tissue in his hand.

The traffic was smooth sailing as the bus merged onto the highway as the sun began to rise up in the now pretty blue sky. It seemed to shine extra bright through his tinted window. Gerald lifted his Tom Ford sunglasses to wipe his eyes, as he settled into his seat and pulled out his phone to listen to some music. He searched through his playlists and found one of his favorite soulful playlists, put his Beats studio headphones on, made himself more comfortable in his seat, closed his eyes and prepared for the long ride. The option to fly would have been much more time efficient and surely more comfortable but the bus ride was what he thought he needed to think and clear his head before attempting to start a whole new life in a new city that he now planned to call home. Every track that played relaxed him even more until he fell asleep. Restlessness overcame him as he saw glimpses of the life, he once shared with Nina over the past ten years and how everything abruptly changed right before his eyes.

He lost track of time between the music and naps until the sound of the bus drivers deep voice came through bus speaker system to announce that they would be making a brief stop in sunny Charlotte, North Carolina. Gerald glanced down at his phone to see if he had enough battery life left to make it the rest of the ride and to see if there were any missed calls or text messages. Relieved but disappointed at the same time neither appeared as he was still waiting for the nightmare to end or it just not be true and also still hoping a message would come from Nina. Playing it all back in his head he recalled the last vision of her while standing in the rear of the church as she was getting ready to say, "I do", to another man that he thought would be himself, only he was too afraid to step up and make himself both emotionally and physically available to be the man she would be able to say "I do" to as he stood there dressed in a navy blue two piece suit which was the last suit she picked out for him to attend the last outing they attended together. The proposal and the beautiful hand-crafted engagement ring he gave her just wasn't enough to keep her any longer for Nina to wait for him to marry her.

The tears began to appear again, and the closing of his eyes forced them to roll down his face. He quickly shook it off, as he was so well known to do and switched to another playlist. The last thing Nina said to Gerald was, "someday the music will stop, the stage lights will go out and you will be standing center stage, alone." He began to wonder, is this that very moment in time that Nina spoke of. The bus pulled into the bus-station and after it came to a stop, he sat there for a few minutes contemplating if he was going to get off for some fresh air and stretch his legs for a few minutes or just sit still in hopes to continue not drawing any attention to himself.

After ten years of being in a relationship that he knew made him the man he was at that moment, no scandals, no mystery kids, no secret affairs… all the things his Mom asked him not to do, he questioned himself how he ended up here in this space in time. Were her final words finally coming to fruition? He was definitely alone and felt like the bright lights had gone out on both his personal and love life. After a few minutes of battling with those thoughts he decided to make his way off the bus to get some of that down south bright sunlight and fresh air while stretching his legs during the brief stop. As he stood there, he saw a young couple that looked like they were saying their farewell just before she boarded her bus. He wondered was it a short time away goodbye or was it the verbal final goodbye that he didn't get from Nina. The warmness of the southern sun shined down on his face while drying his tear ducts behind his dark shades once again. The relocation to Atlanta along with some new collaboration opportunities he was headed to finally would become bittersweet after a year of silence and hiding from the world in the privacy of his condo and when he was spotted out in public he was always hiding behind dark sunshades or tinted windows. Gerald was known to express his hurt through his performances, writing and producing. The many awards he won with and for others as well as himself reflected that he was one of the best in the music writing, performing and producing industry. Right now, he had to face the reality that all the money, cars and houses meant nothing now without Nina by his side. None of those things, could take away the hurt and loneliness he was feeling and drowning in from losing Nina because he just couldn't walk down the aisle and say I do. Something for the first time he really came to the reality that, that was the reason he lost Nina.

The announcement for all passengers to re-board the bus was made so he pulled his baseball cap back down and adjusted his Tom Ford sunshades so that hopefully no one would not recognize him for the rest of the drive down. He re-boarded the bus and as he made his way back to his seat, he saw a copy of the Chicago Tribune newspaper dawning a picture of Nina and her new husband a big business tycoon. He froze like a deer caught in headlights and the older lady who had rode the first half of the ride in the seat next to him grabbed his hand to lead him back to take his seat so she could take her aisle seat. As the bus began to exit the bus station and merged back onto the main road leading to the interstate Gerald placed his headphones back on and closed his eyes hoping he would be able to dose off without another thought or memory of Nina or the photo in the newspaper he had just seen. The sounds of soft jazz put him right back to sleep for what he thought was for hours not long into his nap he drifted into a dream of the evening he met

Nina at the Centerfield Lounge and Bar. The crowd in the lounge were well aware of who Gerald was and the women were a dime a dozen with their eyes on him in hopes that he would at least speak to them but, Nina had no clue who Gerald Livingston was or at least she acted as if she didn't and played the part very well.

Nina was dressed in a tight form fitted Chanel black dress that revealed more curves than even his Lamborghini could handle, leading down to a set of legs only the creator could have blessed her with, move over Tina Turner and Angela Bassett Ms. Nina entered the room. How many squats and hours in the gym did she have to spend to get that ass and them legs he mumbled to himself. The winning attribute for him were her feet in some five-inch Red Bottom heels. He reminisced about the smile she displayed as he lifted his glass from across the room in acknowledgement after she had accepted the drinks, he sent over to her and her party of five. Her smile was so innocent and beautiful, her jet-black hair was cut in a short soft style with highlights of what looked like burgundy wine color, her skin was a soft caramel complexion and a face that was meant for a magazine cover. It was so crowded that night at the lounge that they didn't get to introduce themselves to each other. For weeks he went back just to see if he could catch her there again. Finally, after almost two months later they were at the lounge at the same time and he was too nervous to walk over to speak as she kept blushing making eye contact with Gerald, they were like two teenage kids. After watching them both finally, Mr. Paul stepped in and broke the ice for Gerald by taking them both to an open table and set them up for what they always called their first date, and it was like they were supposed to have met at that moment and not a day before. They laughed and talked for hours until the lounge closed and continued over the phone after she got into the car service, he ordered for her the entire ride to her hotel until the sun came up the next morning.

Nina was a second-year star attorney at one of Chicago's largest law firms, Ashburn and Moxley, out on the town after her team won one of the biggest cases in the firm's thirty-year history. Gerald was an up-and-coming artist in the music industry when they met, so their schedules never seemed to connect in the beginning, but they would spend hours on the phone, talking, video chatting and texting. It was like the first night never ended. Even after learning who Mr. Gerald Livingston the up-and-coming music mogul was, she still treated him like he was just a regular everyday gentleman which was different for him given his growing notoriety and because of that he made himself completely available for her companionship. Nina quickly became the lady to share the spotlight with him in his personal life as well as all over social media and the tabloids. There weren't many times he was spotted out in public without Nina right by his side as the relationship began to grow. The tabloids caught many of their outings together or separate as Gerald's status grew in the industry while all of his music climbed the charts. His career went from being a local talent to a worldwide sensation in what seemed overnight and with all that, still no announcement or buzz from the happy couple about the possibility of a wedding date even after they announced their engagement. The pressure from her family, friends and interviewers began to get the best of them both and eventually drove a wedge between them which added an increased amount of doubt in Nina that, a wedding would ever happen with Gerald. Finally, after ten years of happiness and what seemed to be an inseparable love and what he thought would be a never-ending happiness with Nina, she finally decided it was best for them to go separate ways.

The sound of the bus's airbrakes woke Gerald up along with a soft touch on his hand and a whisper telling him they had finally arrived in sunny Atlanta, Georgia. He sat straight up in his seat trying to wake up and got himself together while the other passengers exited the bus. The little lady who didn't bother him the whole ride down leaned over and whispered again,

"I will tell you this again young man, nobody said a new beginning would be easy" she slipped him some more tissue and got up gesturing him to do the same,

"You can't start if you don't at least walk, Mr. Livingston",

were her next words of comfort and inspiration she offered as she called him by his name and smiled.

"Your next set of steps will only be as bright as the light you allow to shine on them, Mr. Gerald Livingston so lift your head and your spirits."

were the last words she said as she left him seated on the edge of his seat. It was like an angel had been sent from his mom to tell him what she was no longer there to tell him at a moment like this in his life.

CHAPTER 2

"New Start"

AFTER A FEW MORE MINUTES he got himself together then pulled his hat over his brow and adjusted his sunglasses to secure his identity again then he grabbed his leather travel bag making his way to the front of the bus, now that the bus was empty of all the passengers it was just the driver and himself. As he walked to the front of the bus the driver stopped him and whispered,

"It was an honor and a pleasure to have you on my bus Mr. Livingston."

Gerald was always prepared for the request for his autograph, so he searched himself looking for a pen. The driver who appeared to be an older gentleman touched his elbow to stop him and said,

"Sir you owe me nothing and I don't want your autograph, I just want you to get yourself together, we all have to go through a rough and lonely season that we have to endure alone at some point in this thing called life. I want you to move on and take something from this season in your life that will make the next season you are about to embark on ever better. Don't let your past stop you from moving into your future."

Completely shocked and thankful as he held back the tears that began to form, he just took a deep breath and extended his hand for a handshake as he thanked the bus driver. After Gerald thanked the bus driver for not making notice who he was and for extending the kind words he shared with Gerald, he exited the bus to find a seat on a nearby bench and began to try to figure out what his next move would be now that he had arrived in Atlanta. As he sat there watching people walking in and out of the bus station many thoughts raced through his mind of the past year like flipping through the pages of a photo album of his life. The phone rang for the first time since he had left Chicago. Reluctant to take a look and see who was calling he pulled his phone out of his pocket just before the last ring to see the face of his best friend, Chris on the screen. He hesitantly answered expecting an argument or a heated voice on the other end, only to hear the worry and concern in Chris' voice, because Gerald had totally dropped out of the limelight for the last few months and now, he had left Chicago with no notice to anyone. No mention of his plan to leave for any set time or even the thought that he was thinking about completely relocating. Gerald didn't even pack up his rooftop condo and he left all of his cars in the garage. He left everything just like he was just going to the store or something, slipped out on his driver and his security. The doorman didn't even see him leave during the early morning hours. Chris, expressed his concern which eventually switched to disgust and anger, "we have been friends for over thirty-five years G I should have been the one person you told something about your plans to leave. You have Tammy and I worried sick what the fuck man! I know all of this has been hard for you but you just up and fucking leave, damn man!"

There was a long pause after Chris finished, after a long deep breath and sigh before Gerald responded,

"You know what you're right, but I needed to think this one out on my own for a little while and I think I will be gone for a while Chris. I have spoken to a real estate agent here and making plans to purchase a penthouse or a home here in Atlanta which is where I am as we speak. I will be working on my next release, a few collaborations and some business deals here. I am trying to get myself back into the swing of things. I will send for my truck and cars or maybe I will just purchase a convertible to go along with this warm southern weather. Once I am settled in, I will forward you my address until then you can call, text anything of importance or contractual shoot me an email. This is what is best for me Chris, maybe not at this moment but I would hope that eventually you and Tammy will understand. I will more than likely be staying at the Westin like I always do."

They both paused for a brief moment and Chris just expressed his best wishes and told Gerald he would be praying for him. For the first time in their friendship Chris ended the call with Gerald, angry. They always ended their calls with, "You got this, man". It was at that moment Gerald realized he really pissed off the one person who no matter what, always had his best interest in mind. But Gerald knew in his heart this is what was best for him.

Gerald grabbed his bag and made his way out of the bus station with no clue what he was doing next. As the glass doors to the bus station slid open the warmth of the Georgia sun hit his face as it shined through his shades.

Ironically as soon as he stepped through the doors to the left there was a black Lincoln Town Car limo car service available, the style of travel he was accustomed to traveling in. Instead, he flagged down a regular cab and once inside he told the driver simply, downtown on Peachtree and take your time I have plenty of time and money. After an hour of stop and go traffic on a Saturday on the Interstate Eighty-Five they pulled into downtown. Gerald called the only person who really knew he was coming, the real estate agent, Melanie and left a voicemail when she didn't answer, to let her know he was in town and would like to take a look at the penthouse they had discussed at her earliest convenience. The cabdriver asked where he would be staying and if he would need transportation for the remainder of his stay in Atlanta? Almost catching a look at his fares face he had an idea that Gerald must have been somebody famous definitely trying not to be recognized. The driver made him aware that he also owned a limo service that also provided twenty-four-hour service if needed during his stay in Atlanta. Gerald asked for a business card while letting him know he needed to go to the Westin at the Lennox Mall.

After re-adjusting his hat, he requested that the cabdriver pull over so he could make his reservation over the phone. It wasn't his first time staying at The Westin, so when Melanie answered,

"The Westin, this is the front desk, this is Melanie speaking. How may I help you?"

Gerald was relieved.

"Mel it's G can you put me up for a few days and use the card you should have on file?"

There was about a two-minute pause while Mel confirmed she had a private suite reserved for him and instructed him to enter the hotel his normal way, through the garage. Gerald instructed the cabdriver while he finished the check-in with Melanie to proceed to the hotel and to pull into the garage to drop him off. The ride lasted about another ten minutes until they pulled into the garage off of Peachtree St. where Gerald was met by the bellhop Melanie selected to take him up to his suite. As he exited the cab, he requested the cabdriver to return to pick him up in four hours and he would be making multiple stops so be sure he cleared his schedule for rest of the day, sliding the cabdriver the fare along with a one-hundred-dollar tip. The bellhop rushed out to meet him and picked up his bag, by the time the cabdriver turned around Gerald was in the elevator. Once in the elevator the bellhop handed him his key card with his room number on it.

The elevator reached his floor and after they arrived at his suite, he tipped the bellhop and walked into his suite, once again he was alone just like if he was back home, dropped his back at the door, looked around the suite then sat down at the desk in front of the window and looked out at all the people going in and out of the mall. The well-organized valet guys were parking the cars and dashing back to get the next car in line. The ride down to Atlanta on a bus full of people reminded Gerald how lonely he was even surrounded by others, a feeling still fresh since Nina first left him yet he still had to do appearances that had already been scheduled. The phone over on the nightstand rang, it was Melanie checking to make sure everything was to his liking and if he would need anything else, Gerald gave his approval and extended a thank you as well. All he requested was that she not tell anyone he was there, and he would take care of any trouble or inconvenience it may cause her or the staff. Melanie took his request as an insult only because of the many times he had stayed there prior, she could hear something different in his voice from the past times they had spoken during the many stays there before because he wasn't his normal jovial self. She started to make a comment but instead she just agreed to his request and assured his privacy. After their phone call he kicked off his ostrich skin loafers and laid across the bed waiting for a return call from the real estate agent. Afraid to doze off he began to hum a few of his own songs which was also hard to do because most of them were written with his love for Nina in mind. Switching from a hum to singing through a few lines he felt his voice crackling and he knew he would need to definitely do some rehearsing if he planned to get back in the studio any time soon. How long would he hide or how much longer would he hide was the question? The words of the older lady on the bus ride came to mind and like many times before he saved the words on his phone in his notes section because they could possibly become a hook or a line in a song. Still not ready to deal with anybody that could possibly bring up what he was dealing with he immediately closed the screen of his phone, laid back down and rolled over to look up at the ceiling.

The suite phone rang again, this time there was some hesitance to answer but after the third ring he decided to answer, it was Melanie informing him his car was downstairs waiting for him and she would be leaving for the evening but, if he needed anything not to hesitate to call her cell (as she gave him the number) and she would be sure to have it done. She let him know that the bellhop that met him in the garage was assigned to him until she returned in the morning. Gerald repeatedly thanked her and let her know once again how much he appreciated her assistance. At the closing of the call, he let her know he was ready to leave out and she told him the bellhop was already at his door waiting to take him down to his car. He slipped his shoes on and as soon as he opened the door the bellhop was waiting for Gerald in the hallway just like Melanie informed him. Once on the elevator they made their way down to the garage Gerald slipped the bellhop another tip and as the elevator doors opened to his surprise parked with the flashers on was a shiny black Lincoln Town Car with dark tinted windows. The cabdriver was now dressed as a freshly groomed, clean cut limo driver in a black suit, white shirt and black tie as he greeted Gerald while opening the rear passenger side door,

"My name is Sam, Sir. Where will we be headed sir?"

Gerald was both caught by surprise and impressed as he responded,

"There is a change in plans I am only making one stop this evening and that will be to a cigar lounge called, The Highland Cigar Lounge and I will be there for a few hours Mr. Sam."

Once in the car Gerald pulled out his phone to check his schedule which he already knew was free and opened his text messages which were no text or emails now had changed to five new text. He began to scroll through them as if he could hear his mom's voice saying, those message things are not going to open themselves son. Clicking on the first text message was from his manager Joe, of course expressing great concern over wanting to know his whereabouts and warning Gerald if he didn't hear from him within the next twenty-four hours he would be alerting the Chicago authorities. Thinking of the appropriate response he simply text him back, "I am ok, just needed some time away from Chicago. I will be in contact with you sometime tomorrow." Moving onto the next text he opened it was from Mr. Cee as he had called him since he was a little boy which once again expressed concern, "G I know this is and has been a tough time for you, but a lot of people are concerned please just let us know that you are ok, please." is what it read. A quick copy and paste he did of the response to Joe his manager and slowly clicked send. He read a few more and gave the same replies to those as well until the limo division window slid down for Mr. Sam to let him know they had arrived at The Highland Cigar Lounge. Gerald asked for a moment so he could call inside to the owner first he apologized for the short notice of his arrival while letting the owner, Tom know he was actually parked outside and to see if he could be accommodated with a quiet space to have a smoke without being noticed, "of course" the manager/owner Tom said as he made the arrangements while keeping Gerald on the phone while arranging everything so he could let him know when to come in, especially since Gerald was one of his favorite and best customers whenever he was in Atlanta or in Chicago because he ordered cigars to be shipped to him to Chicago as well.

Gerald gave Mr. Sam a head nod to let him know he was ready to go in after Tom let him know everything was set up for him to come in. Mr. Sam was at the rear door to open it for Gerald in a matter of seconds it seemed and once again adjusting his cap as the door was opened for him. Gerald attempted to slip Mr. Sam another nice tip, only to have him refuse it this time.

"Mr. Livingston Sir let me say this, first of all I know who you are, and I will insure as well as respect your privacy. I would like to sincerely thank you for giving my company and I the opportunity to provide your transportation service needs and trusting me to keep your stay here in Atlanta private. I will be parked and waiting for you until you're ready to leave and return to the hotel. As far as a price and contract for my services Sir, we can discuss that at another time once you have cleared your head. If I might add, I have a son your age and I can only imagine what it would feel like to lose the woman you love to someone else. Enjoy your evening and your smoke Sir. I will be waiting right here until you are ready to leave. You have my business card and phone number, and the owner knows me as well so you can have him to call me, or you can give me a call directly whenever you are ready to leave."

Lost for words he swallowed anything else he was going to say about Mr. Sam refusing his tip and responded with simply,

"Thank you, Mr. Sam."

Pulling down his cap and pulling up his jeans as if his mom was there to tell him to straighten himself up as he made his way to the front door of the lounge as he was greeted by the owner Eric and a bar maid as they whisked him through the bar and lounge area to a secluded area already set up with

11

five of his favorite cigars from the Arturo Fuente line on a tray and a glass of his favorite house wine to get him started. The hospitality was always five stars whenever he frequented there after a show or just in town, it was always with Nina on his arm. This time was different, he was alone and no reason for any type of celebratory smoke or toast to be raised tonight. After he sat there for a few moments he made his selection of a cigar which was the Hemingway Classic and what type of cut he wanted as well, he chose to go with a deep V-cut. Taking his time while lighting the cigar with the precision of a well-seasoned cigar smoker being sure to toast it evenly before he put it in his mouth to take the first pull. The first draw and the release of the first puff of huge smoke filled the space he was in as the robust taste and that great smell of the Hemingway calmed the moment as the soft jazz music was playing in the background and although there was a lounge full of conversating and laughing customers, but that moment felt like no one else was in the entire building for those first few minutes.

Gerald took in another full draw letting out a combination of a nice retro-hale and the rest out of the side of his mouth creating another big cloud of smoke and once again he was forced to realize all the money, cars, toys and accomplishments meant nothing without Nina there to share any of it with him. At this time all of his most current songs he sang himself as well as the songs he wrote and produced for others were holding steady at the top spots on the billboard charts, the royalties were coming in for the songs he had even forgotten about, everything he touched seemed to go to the top of the charts and his walls were dressed in the awards as proof of it. But the one person that meant the most to him he couldn't write a song to make her stay until he was ready to say, "I do" or even get her back at this time. Nina was gone and was married to another man who gave her what she wanted from Gerald. Inside he was like a broken glass, outside he was a rare work of art for the world to see and hear through his music. Gerald was now that rare work of art that had no home or cabinet to be placed in, now he was that rare piece of art that was in a gallery waiting for a prospective home to go to. He began to wonder if that was even possible now and it wasn't even because of Nina, he was the problem. Yes, Nina meant the world to him, but he just wouldn't give her what she needed to make life complete with him, she had the unfinished canvas but was missing the frame to put it in and hang it on the wall. Ten years they spent together from their very first date and still no kids or marriage, not even a penciled in date or timeframe was mentioned. Every time she brought up the topic of marriage or starting a family his answer was always the purchase of a new ring with a follow up of another empty promise to talk about it or a new record deal or project was more of a priority than discussing their future which was finished with the time just wasn't the right conversation. He mastered the art of diversion of discussing those subjects and for far too long painfully forcing Nina to finally stamp her own expiration date on the relationship. Only those very close to Gerald knew the real deep-rooted reason why he ran from the idea of marriage. His childhood experiences with a broken family, an absent father and seeing the failed marriage between his parents because of his father's actions now showed its effect on his adulthood. The fear of being like his father cost him the love of his life and now he was wondering if this hurt, he felt was what his Mom felt up until the day she passed away. He was to her what his music was to him only to him the one thing he could do, and it take him away from the pain was his music. She spent her every moment assuring Gerald be successful and nothing like his father to whomever he decided to make Mrs. Livingston. Did he fail his Mom? A question that never surfaced until that moment he sat there alone.

There were times that Gerald spent weeks and sometimes months at a time he would be on the road along with the long hours in the studio and Nina hung in there with him. To make up for the missing time he would spoil her with long extravagant vacations all over the world, surprise expensive gifts, he would take her out on just because shopping excursions in all parts of the world, red carpet walks and weekly flower deliveries to her office, he did everything he thought would make and keep her happy only to finally come home to a three page letter saying goodbye along with the four upgraded engagement rings and last special handcrafted five carat ring that he gave her and never set a wedding date along with any of them. She left everything he had ever given her during their relationship with the exception of the clothes she walked out the door with on her back. The condo still looked like it did the day she had left it a year ago. He even stopped the cleaning service to keep the smell of her in the condo. Nina's voice still sounded so clear in his head so much so he could still hear her on the phone calling to check on him while he was away on tour or an all-nighter in the studio. The time elapsed so long between his last drag of his cigar and his moment of deep thought that it went out. The room was dimly lit, and the haze of smoke made it look like a steamy wet and hot street after a summer rain shower as the streetlights come on and begin to shine down on it. The only thing that was missing was the woman he called his rainbow, Nina.

CHAPTER 3

"Play Time"

AS HE REACHED DOWN FOR his monogramed gold Zikar triple flame lighter he sat back and sparked a flame of fire and slightly leaned in to light his cigar a soft voice spoke softly,

"You'll never finish your cigar like that Mr. Livingston."

The soft voice he somewhat recognized yet startled Gerald because no one was supposed to know he was there at all. Puzzled as he slowly looked up at the small hand to the small wrist wrapped in a classic diamond encrusted Cartier watch which led to a sheer blouse up to the cocoa complexion and the pretty smile of his one-time duet partner, Sandra. A sense of relief as he uttered,

"Hey stranger I have not seen you in almost four years and yes you are right I will not finish my cigar if I keep letting it go out."

After they shared a much-needed laugh for Gerald, Sandra took a seat across from him positioning herself to be sure he couldn't do anything else but to stare at her as he always did when they worked or performed together on numerous occasions. There was always an unaddressed chemistry between the two but out of respect for his relationship with Nina it remained just that, unaddressed. Her presence and smile always made him open up and belt out his strong soulful voice. She crossed her legs and sat sideways so he could get a view of her thick well-maintained thighs down to her sculpted calves leading down to a pair of six-inch open toe Red Bottoms heels showing her freshly pedicured feet and bright red toenails. As she displayed it all for Gerald his eyes were fixated and focused on his cigar as his face quickly turned back to stone which revealed he was back in another space mentally just that fast which helped her to realize it wasn't the time to do anything else flirtatious, so she changed her seating position to a little less sexy and prepared to become more attentive to her clearly lost and troubled friend. Small talk began and like the rest of the world she wanted badly to know what the hell happened with him and his fiancé' Nina, that he always proudly said was his one true soulmate. She leaned in to cut her cigar and lit it in between the breaks in conversation while trying to catch herself from once again from being so obvious with her lustful stares at Gerald. The waitress walked in and placed Sandra's drink on the table that she ordered from the bar. Afterwards the waitress leaned overextending an apology to Gerald from Eric the owner for the unexpected intrusion even after he requested to be in a private room. Eric insisted that Gerald's next round and cigar be on the house but, Gerald refused and told her it really wasn't a problem that Sandra is a good friend and maybe the company wouldn't be a bad idea tonight as he took a second glance at Sandra. Sandra and the waitress both let out a sigh of relief then they both smiled. As the waitress was leaving Gerald and Sandra, he requested some menu's realizing he had not had anything to eat for a few days and he had already taken his first drink for the night on an empty stomach. The waitress suggested the flame broiled turkey burger with a side order of garlic and herb seasoned fries with such anticipation that it made Gerald and Sandra both order it.

Once the waitress left the room Sandra anxiously inquired if he was in Atlanta for business or pleasure and Gerald replied,

"At the moment, I think I will be staying here for a combination of a fresh start and some pleasure then at some point it will be for business but, for now it will be more of a fresh start. Do you think there is enough room down here for one more single man in Atlanta?"

He then looked at her with an innocent boyish smile on his face and they both laughed once again which was something that Gerald really needed much more of especially after that being the first time, he addressed himself as being single without breaking down into tears. Single, a status and a situation that he still had not really come to grips with since Nina left him and even after knowing she was now married, he was actually single again after ten years. Sandra laughed again and commented,

"Wow, it's been almost a year and I am willing to bet that is the first smile you have had both privately and publicly since your last sighting. The last few pictures you that have been taken of you, you wore a frown or a straight face behind some sunshades Gerald, that's not you and you know it. As your friend, I just want to say one thing and nothing else after this if you don't mind. She has left a wonderful man for whatever reason she felt was best for her. We all have our flaws, don't let yours be the reason you totally self-destruct."

Gerald had nothing to say so he just took another pull off of his cigar and smiled at her. After a few minutes he looked at her and softly spoke,

"Still the one with a way with words Ms. Sandra, thank you I needed to hear those words now let's smoke, eat and drink to friendship."

as they raised their glasses, toasted and took a sip while looking through the rim of the glass at each other. Gerald didn't know what to do next and it was clear to Sandra, so she broke the ice by asking where he was staying. He wasn't ready to disclose that information, so he just responded,

"Downtown, until I find a place."

Sandra took the hint and shared she was still in Smyrna,

"I feel like we are yelling can I move closer? As long as I am not overstepping your boundaries."

Sandra asked and Gerald patted the seat next to him with his now sweaty palms. As Sandra grabbed her Prada clutch purse and glass Gerald took another look at her and it sparked some feelings and thoughts he had not felt in over a year. Still, he felt a little guilty even though he was now officially single. Sandra sat down crossed those thick thighs and her blouse dropped enough to show that soft caramel skin leading down to her full cleavage. They engaged into a few hours of conversation over two bottles of wine. The cigars had burned out at this point and she had moved even closer. Gerald was so comfortable her hands moved up and down his back as she now leaned in even further to take in every word of the conversation. He took a glance down at his watch and now realized three hours had gone by and it was at that moment Sandra offered an invitation for a nightcap back at her house, clearly, she shouldn't be driving if she had driven tonight so he accepted and offered her a ride home. When the waitress stuck her head in to check on them, Gerald told her to let Eric know they were ready to leave so he could walk them out while he called Mr. Sam to let him know he was on his way out with an extra passenger. No clue how much the tab would be because he was never able to see one and like the regular routine, he refused to accept the complimentary tab that was always extended so he left three crisp hundred-dollar bills on the table under his glass and another one-hundred-dollar bill for the tip for the waitress under the empty bottle of wine.

As Eric walked Gerald and Sandra along the back wall, he assured Gerald the tab was on the house, Gerald told him he left some cash on the table for the lounge and the waitress and to do as he pleased with it because he would surely be coming back more now because he will be in town for a while. Mr. Sam was parked right out front and ready to take Gerald and his guest back to his suite,

"Change of plans we will be taking my friend home. I have text you the address. Mr. Sam this is Sandra, Sandra this is Mr. Sam."

Gerald informed him as Sandra got in the car. Eric thanked Gerald again, wished him well and welcomed him back to Atlanta as he always did when Gerald would come to the lounge as he entered the car. As soon as the door closed Sandra leaned over to kiss Gerald and with no hesitation, he leaned in to accept the kiss. It was the first kiss or any type of verbal and physical act of affection since, Nina. The feeling of guilt definitely disappeared the way he took her in his arms. She pulled away gently to look at him as her hands made their way over his broad muscular shoulders down to his chest over his ripped abs running over each of them to his thigh before she took a handful of what she had been wanting from the day they first met about four years ago. The heavy breathing, he let escape let her know the nightcap could be one well worth the waiting for, still holding him in her hand she whispered,

"Maybe you should have your driver come back and get you in the morning"

Gerald whispered back,

"I think that is a good idea"

as he leaned in to continue kissing her. Moving his hand over her thigh she opened her leg and let him feel her now wet phatness one finger ran up the middle of her lace boy shorts as she softly moaned his name careful not to let Mr. Sam hear her,

"Gerald…"

She rubbed his sculpted chest and abs again while kissing him on his neck as his hand made its way up to her big firm full breast. Clearly the nervousness was gone and judging by the stiffness in his pants he was ready for what was about to happen as they entered into her gated driveway. Her security guard was thrown off when Mr. Sam opened the door and Gerald got out first giving his hand to Sandra to help her out,

"Good evening Ms. Tomlin will you be needing to be escorted in tonight?"

he asked as she looked at Gerald she replied,

"No, I think I am in very good hands, damn good hands."

Gerald and Sandra entered through the double rod iron doors to her marble foyer that led to a set of dual white marble staircases with gold railings. Not even two steps inside the doors Sandra slipped out of her dress and blouse and afterwards she led Gerald by his now loosened belt to the dimly lit living room where she undressed him slowly while kissing every part of him as his moans drove her crazy, she laid down on her prized African imported leopard skin rug and they kissed passionately until she guided him inside of her wet walls arching her back in total surprise of his first few deep long intense strokes. Her moans escaped her body as her breathing intensified and her body tensed up from the pure pleasure and ecstasy that was shared between the two of them. As the moonlight shined in through the floor to ceiling glass front windows showing his every stroke in a shadow on the wall as she moaned has name over and over again,

"Gerald, Gerald, oh my God Gerald."

It was clear that they both needed what was happening and repeatedly they made love from the living room, to the foyer, on the staircase and for a grand finale to her king size bed until they both fell asleep holding each other.

The sun shined in through the large paned windows in her bedroom while Sandra laid asleep in her bed Gerald got up and stood by the window looking over her grounds and while he watched her two beautiful chocolate brown Doberman Pincher's running freely. He looked over at her sleeping, not an ounce of guilt or that looming loneliness was present. For the first time in a while, he was totally relaxed. Sandra woke up rubbing the space he was supposed to be laying in until he let her know he was in front of the window and made sure she was ok and didn't have a hangover. She looked over at him with a beautiful sexy smile as she patted the bed for him to come lay back down beside her. He accepted her request walked over and laid back down with her she then laid on his chest.

"Are you ok Gerald, is the question I should be asking you?" she asked him.

He replied,

"Actually, I am fine, I needed last night more than you know. I have to admit I was a little nervous at first, but you sure knew how to take that feeling away."

Her maid, Alicia knocked before she entered with the breakfast that he requested while Sandra was asleep. He had some dry toast and a glass of orange juice as he watched her eat a boiled egg and sip on a cup of coffee while looking at how beautiful she was first thing in the morning.

"I am hoping that what happened was mutually desired and not elevated by the alcohol. I have some business to take care of today, but I would love to catch up with later if that is alright with you"

she smiled and responded,

"Such the gentlemen Mr. Livingston. To answer your question, you had me at hello years ago Gerald, now do I wish the timing was different, of course, but everything happens when it is supposed to happen, and I truly believe that. Now come here and give me a kiss before you leave."

A kiss that led to two more hours of passionate love making.

Afterwards they laid there and engaged in more conversation making it clear that there were no expectations at this point for anything on both parts. Sandra had a hair appointment and Gerald needed to get back to his suite to shower and dress for a meeting with Mia the real estate agent to look at a penthouse condo. He called for Mr. Sam to pick him up and within thirty minutes his ride arrived for him. As he was leaving, they engaged in another long kiss that almost led to another session but Gerald pulled her to the door so he could get out of there and not make them both late for their appointments. Once in the car Mr. Sam lowered the partition,

"Good morning Sir, to your suite and then to your agent's office Sir?"

Gerald replied,

"Yes Sir, I see you are very good with following a schedule and attention to detail. I like that and I appreciate it as well."

as he closed his eyes for a much-needed quick nap.

What a first night he had and was sure there would be a few more nights like it to follow with Sandra. Traffic was heavy so his nap turned into thirty minutes of much needed sleep until Mr. Sam awakened him,

"Sir we have arrived at the Westin."

as they pulled into the garage. Gerald then made a call to Melanie to see if his bellboy would be available and she informed him to stay in the car that she would have him there in a few minutes.

"Mr. Sam, I need about forty-five minutes to get showered and dressed for my appointment."

Mr. Sam gave the ok as Gerald was whisked away again to the elevator. Once he was in his suite he stood in the middle of the floor and took a moment to recapture last night. Sandra sent him a text to thank him once again for such a wonderful evening and morning. He responded letting her know the feeling was mutual and then pulled out his clothes for the day luckily, they didn't require any ironing, ironing or anything domestic for the most part were things he hadn't done in a longtime, but he made do. He stepped in the shower and stood there until the water began to get cold before he bathed. Exactly thirty minutes passed, and he was showered and dressed now ready to shop for a place to call his new home. He gave Mia a call to let her know he was on his way to her office and expressed his privacy was very important seeing he was traveling without any security. Dressed in a black Balenciaga sweat suit, white t-shirt and matching sneakers he grabbed his favorite Chicago Cubs baseball cap and out the door back on the elevator to the garage. He text Mr. Sam the address to Mia's office and once Mr. Sam entered it into the GPS he pulled away while Gerald checked his once again overload of both texts/emails and he answered a few until they arrived at Mia's office.

Gerald called up to Mia to let her know he was outside her building and Mia let him know she had her receptionist coming down to bring him up to her office. Mia had experience dealing with high profile clients so she made all the necessary preparations to ensure his privacy by having her receptionist bring him in through the exit door from the hallway so he would avoid being seen by any of the clients in the waiting area. Mia was anxious to meet Gerald in person as she adjusted her fitted dress around her just right thick hips and her blouse to perfectly settle around her perfectly perky breast. As her receptionist entered the office with Gerald, Mia took a deep breath and displayed her business smile as she took a full eye view of Mr. Gerald Livingston in the flesh before she opened her now watering mouth to speak. His physical appearance was nothing like she expected but more than the eye could capture from what she had already seen on the television and pictures he was a well-groomed physical specimen that looked like his arms and legs were about to come out of his black sweat suit.

"Mr. Livingston, nice to finally meet you in person and put a face and a voice behind the text and emails. I have scheduled some showings for a few properties for us to see today and if we are unable to find you something today, I have a few scheduled for tomorrow as well. How much time do we have today because a few of them are a distance apart from each other?" Gerald was just as amazed with Mia's aura and her body as she was with his,

"I have freed my schedule for the entire day and I have a car service available for us as well"

Gerald told her as they exited the office again through the side entrance to the elevator. They had some light conversation about his plan to transition to Atlanta as they entered the elevator until they exited into the busy lobby and there were a few stares which of course led to someone in the crowded lobby recognizing Gerald and that turned into him being surrounded by some fans and signing some autographs for a few minutes until Gerald was able to excuse himself and they headed out through the revolving doors straight to the car with his hand on the small of her back. Mia wasn't sure if she wanted to walk fast or take her time to enjoy the firmness of his big strong hand. Once they were in the car, Mia gave Mr. Sam the addresses in the order they would be viewing the properties and handed Gerald her iPad so he could see some photos of the first property they were to go to see. She jokingly said,

"I am sure traveling without security is new to you but, you handled that quite well."

Gerald never looked up from the iPad he just smiled and nodded his head as he spoke softly, you are absolutely correct. Mia's appearance made it hard for him to pay attention to the iPad with the movement of her manicured bright red painted nails to show him the selling points of the property on the screen that were connected to her small hands showing the beautiful skin tone of her hands as he looked up to the beautiful smile which encased her perfectly white teeth behind her full lips that were highlighted with red Mac lipstick that perfectly covered her lips down to her soft bright light skin complexion revealing her exposed cleavage from her leaning forward to show him all of the highlights of a single family home in a gated community that they were headed to see first. She was trying not to stare hard as well, and she was able to stay focused with the business at hand by answering each of Gerald's questions. As they arrived at the first property to view the fifty-four hundred square foot single family home. Mr. Sam backed into the driveway and got out to open the door for Gerald and Mia to go inside to take a tour of the huge brick front house.

Once they were inside while walking through each room of the house Gerald watched her ass and every movement she made, and he listened closely to her every word to be sure to remember everything she said. The home and grounds were immaculate, but the house was more than Gerald needed or wanted at the time considering he would be moving there alone. Mia made him so nervous, his palms were sweating as he felt her looking at him as much as he was looking at her, would this be a part two of his first night in Atlanta with Sandra. As they exited the house, he suggested they grab some lunch after they toured the next property and with a big smile, she accepted his invite. They got back into the car and headed to the next property which was a condo that she showed him some pictures of until they pulled into the underground parking garage. While they were on the elevator, she gave him a run-down of all the amenities that came with living in the building until the elevator stopped at their floor which was located on the eighteenth floor which exited right at the front door of the condo. While Gerald walked ahead of Mia she made reservations for lunch at a café she had an idea that Gerald just might like and forwarded the address to Gerald so that he could let Mr. Sam know where their next stop would be. This condo was everything Gerald was looking for until she took him to the next property which was the rooftop penthouse condo in the same building. Every room they went in sold Gerald to the point that they were talking about color schemes, what type of furniture and art work he could put in there, how he could arrange the furniture and where he could purchase the pieces for what he was now calling his new Atlanta home. Laughter filled the rooms and the deal was pretty much sealed but the intensity could be felt from them both during the conversation which changed from closing the deal to some personal question and answer about each other for about an hour as they stood in the gourmet styled kitchen which featured a six burner stainless steel stove, stainless steel appliances with a sub-zero side-by-side refrigerator finished with a black marble granite counter top, white lit frosted glass door cabinets and beautiful glass drop lighting. Mia could feel the mood shift in the conversation from both of them so she grabbed Gerald's hand to show him more of the penthouse which eventually lead to the exchange of a kiss as they stood in the oversized master suite in front of the fireplace. Their kiss was interrupted by a phone from Mr. Sam called to remind Gerald it was nearing the time for their lunch reservations, Gerald stopped long enough to give a quick response while Mia continued to kiss him trying to make sure her heavy breathing couldn't be heard through the phone from the intense caressing of her body as he now pressed her up against the wall next to the fireplace. The phone call didn't stop or slow the passionate kiss which led to her unzipping his sweat jacket and her hands went up under his t-shirt rubbing all over his abs up to his firm pecks over his now erect nipples while he kissed her on the neck. His hands moved over curvy body stopping at her ass as he caressed both of her firm plump cheeks in his hands. She moaned softly knowing that they shouldn't be doing this, but her hands said something else as she pulled him back into her arms while she continued to kiss him. He followed her lead as she began to unbutton her blouse now standing in front of him so he could get a good look at her. After the last button was unfastened she asked him was ok, and the kissing started again which was his answer to her question and they continued undressing each other with heavy breathing and passion once her skirt was down to her feet he turned her around and kissed her on her neck and took a handful of both her breast while rubbing her nipples until she reached around rubbed his big hard dick slowly leaning over far enough for her to take him inside of her now wet walls as she put her hands on the wall to push back on his dick. Gerald went to work on her until her nails clawed the wall and she let off a loud moan and purred out, she was about to cum. Not long after she orgasmed, he went into a serious deep stroking mode until he pulled out and also moaned out he was about to cum. Her now weak knees caused her to lean against the wall forehead pressed against the wall until she could get herself somewhat together then she turned around only to see he was still erect because he didn't cum. She looked at him and said,

"Now we can't leave you and him like that sir."

As she leaned in to kiss him again and began massaging his dick at the same time which led to the some more heavy breathing and finish undressing each other as they made their way out on the deck the clothes were scattered across the floor in a trail from the master suite to the terrace in different places where they tried to stop themselves, but the intensity was just too strong. Neither seemed to be worried about getting caught by anyone or being seen by someone in any of the other adjacent buildings. The intensity was so strong as he held her from behind their two naked bodies formed like an ice sculpture about to melt as she climaxed again just as he entered her craving body. This was unbelievable to Gerald and definitely out of the normal for the always professional Mia who was very conservative up until that very moment and knowing this it didn't stop neither one of them. They made love on the rooftop terrace like they had known each other before today because Gerald seemed to know her every hot spot as well as just what each one needed and when it needed to be attended to as well. She turned around to look him in his eyes as she pushed him back so she could straddle him on the cushioned chaise that was there for staging and immediately she climaxed harder than the first two times as she intensely rested her palms on his now tight chest to position herself to be able to grind him deeper inside of her. Moans of passion came from both of them until she climaxed yet again, without pausing after her orgasm she kept grinding him again until he groaned and pulled her down to hold her as he climaxed as well. After an hour of unexpected passion, it hit them both that they were naked on the terrace in broad day light, so they jumped up and went inside and collapsed on the living room floor in front of the oversized sliding glass doors. Both were amazed with what had just happened as they just laid there side by side looking up at the ceiling both still breathing heavy. Mia rolled over and reached for her blouse and covered her chest while nervously but totally pleased with what had just happened while chuckling a little while repeating, "Wow, wow...wow." She made small conversation and Gerald was listening but was surely lost in the moment and Mia did her best to try to stay focused without looking down his amazing big dick again. Mia got up first and pulled at Gerald to follow her to pick up their trail of clothes so they could get dressed and they did pretty good until Mia bent over to pick up her lace black boy-shorts and it was on again in the master bedroom for one more round of hot passion. After another fifteen minutes they were finally able to get it together, luckily there was a few toiletries in the master bathroom for them to freshen up and head out to a now much needed lunch. The body language changed between the two and Mr. Sam could tell by the way Gerald stood in between him and the car door to assist Mia out himself. When she stood up, she looked like a tall glass of wine to everyone walking by including Mr. Sam who stepped aside as Gerald helped her step up on the curb.

Once they were inside the restaurant and seated without Gerald being recognized there was some talk about business and the future penthouse, he would soon call home. Mia hesitantly shared her current relationship status which was, separated after Gerald asked, not expecting him to open up about his relationship status although it was already known and had been published in all the tabloids. The mood of the lunch date was like two people getting to know each other beyond the business aspect. Gerald was limited with what he shared but with what he did share she knew he wasn't looking for anything or anyone right now and given her current relationship status neither could she. Still in shock by the earlier event she still couldn't believe she melted under such intensity but was surprisingly relaxed because Gerald seemed so different than the past and present vultures who tried their hand with her. Finally, they got back to discussing the paperwork for the penthouse that he decided was definitely the one he was going to make his Atlanta home, it was actually similar to his condo he had back in Chicago. They also discussed finding a space for a studio as well and after an hour and a half of talking business over smoked salmon salads and wine they headed back to her office to do the paperwork for the penthouse while trying to keep it professional but, if one of them slipped it would be another terrace session right there in her office. After they made it through the completion of the paperwork, they bid each other goodbye with a handshake that still held the intensity that was created the moment he walked in her office over eight hours before. Gerald let her know that the penthouse was a done deal, and they could talk later in the evening if she was free. She walked him out to the side door to the elevator this time there was a soft professional hug exchanged. As he entered the elevator, he turned around looked at her with a smile as the elevator doors closed, he thought to himself damn, another Georgia Peach in less than forty-eight hours of his arrival in Atlanta, is this what the single life would be like and once again there were no thoughts of Nina. Gerald thought could this have been what he needed after Nina left him instead of hiding from the world as he checked his phone which was full of new and unanswered text and emails from earlier. He was exhausted from yet another unexpected steamy sexual encounter he dozed off in the backseat with his phone still in his hand, while on the way back to his suite.

Mr. Sam woke him up just before they arrived back at the hotel so he could call to let Melanie know he was about ten minutes away so the bellhop would be available to take him up to his room for a shower and he was sure to pass out afterwards. He had seen more people and physical interaction in two days than he had in a year because he went into hiding.

Melanie called not long after he was out of the shower and had dozed off to make sure housekeeping had dropped off the extra pillows and towels, he requested. She made some small talk about him being in and out since he checked in and they both laughed as he told her he was trying to get his life in some type of order and that he found a place to live since he would be moving to Atlanta for good if everything went well. The conversation went from a customer service call to yet another nightcap invitation from Gerald as a thank you for her assistance. All of his working out and overload on supplements were proving their effectiveness for sure.

"So, Melanie what are you doing when your shift ends tonight? Home to the man? I am sorry if I have overstepped my bounds."

As he chuckled a little and there was some hesitation and finally Melanie responded nervously,

"No Mr. Livingston...no man and no kids just lil ole me and my plants"

they both laughed and a short silence came over the phone, again. Gerald really wasn't sure if he had overstepped his bounds by asking about her personal life so he was just as nervous about what her response to his invitation would be as she was to give her answer but, it was too late, so he just blurted out his invitation,

"Melanie if you're not busy maybe we can grab a bite to eat when you get off this evening? Just a show of my appreciation for all of your help both past and present. You have been a great help with my stays here."

A little nervous chuckle from the other end of the phone at first then Melanie accepted the invitation and made the suggestion that they order something from the restaurant downstairs in the hotel knowing how much he wanted to avoid the possibility of being spotted out somewhere she so rethought her suggestion, at the same time in her mind, she thought of what she could cook for him.

See you around eight Mr. Livingston she confirmed while she was trying to keep her composure and not let the blushing on her face seem so evident because she was at the front desk in front of customers and staff. Gerald accepted and after they hung up, he fell back on the bed with his arms wide open relieved that she didn't decline or take it personal that he inquired about her personal life but at the same time he was filled with mixed feelings in his mind as he questioned himself if he was doing something wrong. He was tempted to call her back with an excuse to cancel until he once again remembered, he was single. Gerald was definitely tired from the night before and the sexual escapade while home shopping. He laid there looking up at the ceiling until he fell into a deep sleep which was some much-needed rest for a few hours before Melanie would be arriving.

Five taps on the door woke him up which was the signal established for both housekeeping and his bellboy, Gerald woke up and slowly sat up sitting there for a second before he got up and walked over to open the door looking through the peep hole to see that it was Melanie. When he opened the door and saw a dressed down Melanie he paused because she was dressed in some black leggings, t-shirt and some lip gloss, simple but beautiful. It was a shock to him because he had never seen her in anything other than her uniform behind the front desk. Lost for words he blurted out the first thing that came to his mind based off of what his eyes could see,

"Damn Melanie, so this is what you look like when you aren't charming the gentlemen from behind the counter with that pretty smile."

She just smiled then blushed as she shook her head and asked him was he ready to eat as she gestured him over to the table by the window so they could eat the meal she brought in with her.

"Have a seat and let me set the table for us to eat some dinner. I knew you really didn't want to leave the room and chance being seen."

All he could focus on was her long hair that was out of the bun she always wore at the front desk that was now draped over her shoulders, her caramel complected skin and a plump ass that had definitely been tucked away under her uniforms and behind the front desk. He sat down as she laid out the spread, which was homemade stuffing stuffed chicken breast, homemade mash potatoes, steamed asparagus, bottles of chilled Fiji water and a bottle of white wine. She came fully prepared with plates, silverware, wine glasses and glasses for the water as well and some fine white cloth napkins. Gerald watched her as she moved around making preparations for them to eat, he commented,

"This looks home cooked, Melanie. You have surely outdone yourself. We could have gone down to the restaurant but thank you because I cannot remember the last time, I have had a home cooked meal. You probably didn't want to be seen with me anyway."

With a little smirk grin on his face and Melanie with a little sarcasm responded,

"Really Mr. Livingston, why wouldn't I want to be seen with you? Other than it goes against the rules and regulations of my employer and yes, it is all home-cooked I went home first. Do you realize what time it is and how long you must have been asleep sleepyhead? It's all over your face I woke you up, I am so sorry."

He took a glance down at his diamond encrusted Cartier watch and all he could do was shake his head as he gestured her to join hands for prayer before he would dig into this beautifully prepared home cooked meal. The beginning of the meal was quiet because he dove into his plate like someone who hadn't eaten some good home cooked food in a longtime because it was true. After he came up for air and Melanie teased him about how he was devouring his food then they had a conversation about his plans to make Atlanta his new home, his career and he even opened up about the failed relationship that landed him there to Atlanta. The conversation was both refreshing and insightful for them both, more so for Melanie because all she knew was the Mr. Livingston who was whisked by the front desk or through the garage entrance. Hours had gone by after they had finished eating and Melanie cleared the table. They moved the conversation on the sofa Mia sat with her legs crossed with her arm resting on the back of the sofa as her hand rested on his shoulder while watching television. Not much longer into the conversation Mia's head rested on Gerald's shoulder and they both fell asleep while the television watched them. Melanie woke up about an hour later, quietly got up and gathered her shoes and moved her bag of eating utensils to the door afterwards she walked over to drape a blanket over Gerald before she planned to leave, as she grabbed the door handle Gerald mumbled,

"So, you just going to fill my belly and then leave me without at least saying goodbye, that is just rude."

In a jovial way as he displayed a big smile on his face.

Melanie stopped dead in her tracks looking at the door before she turned around and nervously, she walked back over to Gerald who was now standing up with his arms open waiting for a hug. She didn't have her shoes on which made her even shorter, much shorter than Gerald she dropped her shoes as she walked over to him and leaned into give him a hug. The hug was long and soothing to them as they both released a deep silent sigh. Melanie hands slowly moved up his muscular back as she now let out a soft sigh that he could hear and feel as her body went limp in his arms this time. She made a slight attempt to let go but Gerald wrapped his long muscular arms around a little tighter as he pulled her in closer and both of them were unsure what the next move should be so Melanie lifted her head up to look Gerald in his eyes and as she was about to say something only to be met by his lips for a soft kiss. They both stopped and she laid her head on his chest. Gerald whispered in her ear was she ok her response was evident when she looked back up at him and extended her lips to his for another kiss that led to more passionate kisses in between gasp of air before the next kiss as they began to undress each other slowly. Gerald began to pull back, but Melanie pulled him back in each time he would try to pull away showing him she wanted him just as passionately as his kisses he gave her that started the encounter and it didn't take much for him to show her he wanted her too. Her hands went down to finish loosening his already falling pajama pants as they fell to the floor she slid her hand down inside of his boxer briefs to be greeted by something she hadn't felt or even seen in a long while, she rubbed and stroked his big dick right out of his boxers as she sat him down on the bed in front of him. All at once she took his dick in her mouth deeply and intensely as the sound of passionate moans filled the suite from both of them. Their bodies looked like a piece of beautiful black erotic artwork. She looked up at him as she worked on him like a medic on a 911 resuscitation call and her patient was very responsive to her tending care. Every time he tried to pull her up she would take his dick all the way in her mouth as she looked up at him she did more mouth to dick resuscitation. Ten minutes into it he finally was able to pull away from jaws of life and his well-defined abs relaxed as he laid her back on the bed and his face looked like he was in total disbelief as she looked up at him. She didn't let the change of positioning stop her as she took control back and rolled him over so she could go right back to work on her new friend for the night at least while her hands and lips kissed him from his lips to his neck over his chest down to his perfectly carved abs down to her new mouthpiece that she slowly took deep in her mouth. As Gerald neared his climax she slowed down because she wasn't ready for it to happen and surely, he didn't want it to happen so soon. She came up for air and worked her way up kissing his now tensed body all the way back up until she got to his lips again. Gerald found some strength to roll her over and took a look at her beautiful body that had been under her uniform and hidden behind the front desk all this time. He kissed her from her lips to her neck around to her ear as he breathed heavy and moaned so she could hear him then back to her lips while his one hand rubbed her firm full breast prepping her now stiff nipples and the other under the middle of her back before he made his way down to suck on them as she gasped for air and gripped the sheets in both hands while she tried to ask him was he sure he was ready... her answer came when he looked her right in her eyes before he went down to her now half worn pink lace boy shorts slowly spreading her firm thick thighs after sliding them to the side and running his tongue up and down her now wet, throbbing and fat pretty pussy lips before he pulled them off to see her well-groomed pussy so he could separate them to softly but intensely lick and suck on her clit along with slow deep intense tongue lashes. The sounds of her wet pussy increased the volume of the sounds of passion that escaped from her as she took another two handfuls of the sheets and pulled them as her body arched into an almost perfect C with nothing touching the bed but the crown of her head and tips of her toes. He ate her pussy like a man on a mission to please with unbelievable skills that definitely revealed no signs of rust after his year away from any physical or verbal contact at all with a woman and some much-needed attention she hadn't experienced in so long she had forgotten how good it could feel. She moved and squirmed in fear he would find her hot spot, which didn't work because not long into his intense assault she let out a sexy moan and cried out,

"Gerald...Gerald...Gerald, I am about to...I am about to...I am about to cum, oh FUCK Gerald!"

and her cry was the signal that made him apply more intensity to make sure she not only orgasmed but that she would cum hard and when she did, she came so hard her body collapsed then began shaking so hard it was almost like Gerald could see her actual heart racing from the up and down movement of her chest and her heavy breathing was surely proof. She reached down and pulled him back up to kiss her while she licked her juices off of his lips at the same time. Gerald was lost and at the same time caught up in ecstasy at the same time as she rolled back over to regain her control from him as she made her way back down to his big vein exposed hard dick to finish what she started first. Gerald reached for his travel bag on the nightstand and pulled out some condoms while he tried to continue to watch her take all of him inside of her mouth and she returned his watching eyes with hers dead locked into his eyes as well. In a very sexy way, she nodded her head in agreement with just the head of his dick resting just at the tip of her lips as she glanced over at the condom in his hand then she went back down it slow and intense before she reached up to take the now opened pack from him. It was like the green light for her to put the pedal to the metal now that her patient was requesting and requiring the next step to the treatment she was administering. She took the condom out of the pack while she stroked down onto his dick as looked up at him whispering are you ready as she kept it in her hand while she made her way up to straddle him inside of her up and down a little at a time while slowly working him all the way inside of her trying to avoid the inevitable, but it didn't work as she paused and climaxed once again. The light from the tv with no volume made it look like a dim lit scene from a romantic yet erotic scene, when he saw her silhouette on the wall its mesmerized Gerald as he reached around her soft hips to grab her phat ass with both hands to control her now intense grinds as her moans and sounds of passion continued to resonate in the room.

Her hands were firmly planted on his well-defined pecks so much so she was sure to leave her finger prints in his skin as she worked her hips in a slow intense motion and she once more climaxed as she moaned out his name just before he rolled her over on her back without taking his dick out his first stroke was like he re-entered all over again so he could hear her gasp again as he went in deeper with each stroke, "Ummmm Melanie," is all he could whisper repeatedly as her body convulsed intensely until she climaxed again. Like the rhythm of one of his best pieces he composed another masterpiece inside of her now perfectly fitting drenched throbbing walls. He laid down over her now sweaty body while kissing her passionately continuing his intense but passionate assault on her until he lifted back up while lifting her legs then he held them together and slowly turned her on her side and she looked back at him in total amazement as he created another masterpiece in her walls while he slowly stroked her he lowered down to kiss her some more until he moaned out,

"Melanie, I am about to…shit I am about to…I can't hold it…shit!!"

At that moment he went in like a patient who had been revived and they both climaxed intensely together, and he collapsed behind her. Both of them were unable to move so he laid down behind her and grabbed her then he held her tightly, they were both at a loss for words, so they just laid there and let silence fill the air. Melanie closed her eyes for a few minutes which seemed like eternity until she finally got up the nerve to ask him,

"Gerald…What just happened? I have never done anything like this before. You were absolutely amazing. I promise you I won't turn into some crazy stalker or anything like that…wow. I sure hope this won't be the last time I can share such an experience like that with you. Should I leave now? Really, what just happened? I know I am rambling. I am sorry."

Gerald realized she was in shock and she really was rambling, so he just pulled her in tight again, pleased but confused at the same time with no answers to offer her because he really didn't have any. After a few minutes of holding her with his eyes closed he just told her everything was ok and to just relax.

His mind was racing and full of confusion at this moment, he hadn't been in Atlanta for three full days and already he had slept with Sandra, Mia and now Melanie. Gerald hadn't been with anyone at all since meeting Nina and the entire ten years they were together including the entire year after she left him and broke his heart it seemed like he was recklessly making up for lost time. They laid there and just looked at the lights shining in from outside until they both dozed off in that same position.

Morning came and Gerald jumped up worried Melanie would be late for work and he would be late for his twelve o'clock meeting with Mia only to find she had showered, dressed and already ordered him some coffee and breakfast from the kitchen, benefits of being the front desk manager. Although it was still awkward for them both they hugged, kissed and made a plans for a date later in the evening. Melanie stood there for a few seconds just looking at Gerald clearly, she had some questions about last night, but she said she would just let it be for now, she too had been single for over a year from a married boyfriend whom she didn't know was married until the day she met the wife when she checked in at the front desk for a women's conference when checked in using his credit card. Melanie gave it another shot at expressing herself before leaving out to go home and get ready for work,

"Please don't make a fool of me and please be upfront with me. I have already had that to happen to me. I just want you to know and fully understand that what happened last night was very much needed and unexpected but wanted but, I can be your Melanie at the front desk and nothing else if that is what's best for you. My intentions were not to confuse you or myself."

Gerald responded short and firm while pointing at the door in his stern business voice,

"Like yourself I didn't expect what happened and if I have done anything that has offended you please accept my apology. With that being said, I want to see you tonight no, I am expecting to see you tonight Melanie."

With a smile on her face changing her posture from Mel and now sounding like his personal contact at the front desk, Melanie sarcastically responded as she walked out the door,

"Your car will be here at eleven o'clock as you requested Sir, downtown traffic can be tough especially on a Saturday morning and I believe you mentioned your appointment is at twelve o'clock so make sure you are on time, Sir."

They both laughed as she closed the door as he tossed a pillow at her. He got up to eat the breakfast and sip the coffee she ordered while he was checking his text and emails. Still nothing from Nina or Chris just the normal messages requesting his services and now his itinerary for the day popped up, something he hadn't had in quite a while, an itinerary. Not only did he have an itinerary, but he actually remembered how to make one. Unaware Jay his first cousin and protector since they were kids and official security since day one of his star status now had arrived in Atlanta due to Chris telling him where Gerald had run off until there was a hard knock on the door that sounded like the person on the other side was trying to come through the door. He automatically knew who it was as he answered the door to the large framed Jay that barely could make it through the doorway without turning sideways. Immediately Jay bear hugged him and then laid into Gerald for leaving in the middle of the night without any security and making him look bad as his security more importantly as his cousin. Jay made a promise to his Aunt, Gerald's mom that he would take care of Gerald and he was dedicated to making sure he kept his word. After his speech and another bear hug it was business as usual as he took Gerald's phone to read over the itinerary for the day while Gerald finished his breakfast and coffee.

They talked about his bus trip down and what Gerald had done since he had arrived in Atlanta. Shocked that Gerald actually caught a bus and happy that he was safe at the same time Jay told him,

"Cousin, glad you have broken out of that shell you put yourself in after Nina left you but, you know you need to slow down."

Jay wasn't even looking at Gerald when he said what he felt had to be said as he looked out the window while he called Chris to let him know he was in the room with Gerald and not to worry he was staying with him until he figured out what he is going to do. Gerald felt a feeling of calmness come over him that this move may just workout for him now that Jay was there and especially now that he may have begun to shake the year-long loneliness he swallowed himself up in. Gerald finished his breakfast and headed into the shower as he let Jay know it was good to see him and to have him back by his side.

Standing in front of the mirror as he shaved his head and lined his beard and mustache up, he tried to figure out how he was able to perform back-to-back with two beautiful women in less than three days. Melanie was a definite surprise as he could still smell her on his mustache. Realizing the time was slipping away he made his way into the shower. As he stood in the shower and just let the water run over his freshly shaved bald head knowing he had to see Mia today it had only been twenty-four hours since he saw her and the flashback of them making love on the terrace like two sex craving addicts. All he could think of was her amazing tall slim frame but packed just right with a beautiful personality to match. Her major flaw for him was the fact that she was still married, separated but married. He wondered if he would be able to see her and not want to repeat their last encounter. The shower water felt so good on his muscular body and his freshly bald head, but he recognized the time was slipping away so he washed and got out.

Showered and now dressed in some casual attire some Seven jeans, Polo T-shirt a pair of his favorite charcoal gray and black Nike Air-Max 95's for the day and then came the knock on the wall outside of the bathroom from Jay, "Boss you ready?" that deep voice he missed but one that he knew would keep him in line now that he was there in Atlanta with him. Gerald opened the already cracked open bathroom door. Although Jay knew his one and only responsibility was too secure Gerald, he was family, so he knew him very well, but he didn't let that interfere with him doing his job. That being said he knew he had some room to say some things others couldn't and now was one of them times he did as they now entered the elevator,

"Gerald you have been here in Atlanta less than a weeks-time and you have already slept with three women, I know you are single now and you are trying to get yourself together from the hurt of losing Nina, but you have been successful with no drama in your career so far so please don't start it now. I have prided myself for being able to shield you from that, please don't let me down, now."

As usual somewhat respecting the ten-year age difference and of course his massive frame but most importantly Jay's wisdom Gerald's response was,

"I know and thank you Jay. It has been an emotional rollercoaster since… (then he paused) Nina. I just came here to get away from all of the memories and get a fresh start. I will slow down Cousin, I will slow down."

Jay laid one of his massive hands-on Gerald's back as a sign of accepting what Gerald had to say and afterwards nothing else was said because Gerald knew Jay had his best interest in mind. Now that Jay was back Mr. Sam was waiting out front as the elevator stopped at the front door of the hotel and as they exited Gerald glanced over at the front desk looking for Melanie, there she was with her smile greeting a customer. He winked and pointed at his watch and she looked at hers as well with a big smile on her face. Jay did his normal hand in Gerald's lower back to signal him to move it along as people in the lobby whispered, is that Gerald Livingston, Jay whispered, we have eyes and Gerald regained his focus as they whisked out the door straight to the limo where Mr. Sam was standing at the opened rear limo door waiting for them. Once they were in the limo the partition glass lowered as Mr. Sam greeted Gerald,

"Good morning, Sir has there been any changes to the itinerary for today?"

Gerald confirmed there were no changes as he answered some more of his emails and texts. News seemed to travel fast that Gerald was back out and moving around judging by the text and emails. Gerald was focused but still feeling the tense movements of Jay, so he looked up and said,

"Jay, relax man, this is the most I have done and been out in a year. I will do my best to slow down with these women. It's not like I set out to meet and have sex with these women, hell if that was the case, I could have just paid an escort service for that much…damn. At some point I want to date again but nothing serious right now, ok. Yes, you're absolutely right I haven't had any drama or controversy at least until she left me and got fucking married to the first dude she met behind my back."

Jay looked over at Gerald with a raised eyebrow and held his phone down for a minute because that was the first firm response about Nina's leaving in a year. If it wasn't a sad short response it was no response at all. There was nothing else said from either of them after that just their heads down to their phones.

A few minutes later Gerald's phone rang, and it was Sandra, there was a flirtatious exchange that was quickly followed by an invitation to a night of dinner and a challenge to rematch of the tap out session that Gerald delivered their first steamy night together. Jay once again lifted his head as Gerald told her there would definitely be another night like their first night, but he would have to see what his schedule would look like for the rest of the week. Sandra was in total agreement with that and moved onto the business side of the conversation and she ran through a few lines of some music she had been working on to him. Gerald was a sucker for music as she sang something that caught his attention. Jay knew the closing of his eyes and look on his face too well and his response after she finished was proof when he came out of his short musical trance and responded with excitement Jay hadn't seen in a while,

"You got something there, work on the hook and we will surely be getting together this week to work on that piece you just sang, ok."

Sandra with great excitement agreed and ended the call with something that made Gerald smile even harder than when he answered the call. The car slowed down as Mr. Sam lowered the partition glass to let them know the destination was five minutes away on the right. Jay doing his security looked around and told Mr. Sam to pull over in front of the handicap curb entrance sign. Mia was standing in front of the tall, tinted glass entrance with her over the shoulder black Coach Messenger bag waiting for them to pull up while looking at her phone until she noticed the car pulling up. Today, even Mr. Sam said to himself damn look at the legs on this lady as she walked out to the car. Jay relieved Mr. Sam of his duties by meeting her at the curb to assist her into the car to join Gerald on the same seat next to Gerald who looked up long enough with a blushing smile to greet her as he continued to respond to his emails. The sexual tension was surely on high alert as they both looked each other over as she talked to him about the properties she had located and updated him on the status of the penthouse.

The rest of the day was spent looking at multiple properties to possibly buy and sell as well as a studio space for Gerald. There was definitely a strong sense of tension in the air that was nothing but sexual desire from the both of them but doing his job and doing it well by knowing his Cousin, Jay was able to get control of Gerald's portion of it at least while they were in the car. But today was different because although he wanted more of Mia's loving, the more he wanted the more Jay's words sank in his brain that he needed to slow down before this became a mess between these three women and himself. The call that the penthouse deal was done as well as an offer had been confirmed and accepted on two other properties within minutes after they looked at them made the deal even sweeter having Mia as an agent. Going against his strong beliefs of no business and pleasure he was very attracted to Mia and it would be a problem hiding it when Jay wasn't around. How did he get here in just a few days he wondered as they returned back to Mia's office? No feelings of guilt and not even a thought of Nina but honestly, he knew that in order for anything to remain a fresh start he needed to somehow put the brakes on all of them, but he knew outside of the possibility of confusion and someone eventually getting hurt he was really having a good time with the thought that these three women were interested in him.

Gerald and Mia went up to her office to do the contracts and of course some small talk about the day they spent together and how they were both able to control their urge to recreate the penthouse scene again which almost led to another encounter right there in her office until Jay called him to see how much longer he would need. Gerald snapped out of it and Mia was able to focus back on the business at hand. This could definitely be a power unit because Mia was good at what she did and didn't waste time getting anything done. In three days, she had contracts on four properties and a closing date for his penthouse. Everything was falling into place, now if he could avoid falling between her legs again to fully regain his focus things would be even better. The paperwork was finished and like a clean prison break he escaped without being caught again. Out of her office and in the car, he headed back to his suite for now what he needed, some very much needed rest and quiet time to think things out at some point, something he hadn't really done since he arrived in Atlanta.

CHAPTER 4

"Decisions"

IT HAD BEEN ALMOST THREE months now since he moved into his penthouse and closed on about five other properties and a few other business ventures were in the working. The penthouse was almost fully furnished, and he was still maintaining the three women only now he was starting to feel the emptiness he was running from when he left Chicago. Gerald laid in the bed looking up at the ceiling with his headphones on and thoughts were circling around in his head, all that he had going on which was what he had created both the good and not so good in regard to the women in his life. Properties and ventures closing faster than Mia's legs were. A friendship that was on the verge of being called a relationship. What was supposed to be a business relationship turned into weekly dinner date nights, lunch dates, a few trips to exotic places and their favorite getaways were to different furniture stores. The only deciding factor stopping it was the fact that she was still married and seemed to still be fighting with leftover feelings for her husband although she was hurt but clearly, she hadn't let go of him or the marriage. There were moments that she was all in with Gerald then there were moments she would be distant when it came to both the past and present personal sides of her life. Feelings he could fully understood and identify with because he too still was battling with some unresolved feelings and emotions for Nina. As a team they worked well in business and between the sheets but how much longer would that last before someone slipped completely on the feelings beyond business. Would it be Gerald as a rebound from Nina or would it be Mia because Gerald was everything, she had hopes her now estranged husband should have been after seven years of marriage.

There was Sandra who in no way was ready to let up off of the gas pedal as far as career wise or the pursuit of a relationship with Gerald. If nothing else she was going to stay just to see if she could conquer him sexually. She had a voice that seemed to melt Gerald in front of a mic and in his ear. Harmoniously they worked together in music and their duets were the sounds and of two in love. The past few months she had been back in the studio and the buzz was out that she would be releasing another single under Gerald's label and guidance. The record labels were coming out of the woodworks for her but tucked away under Gerald's guidance she wouldn't make a move without him. She knew the life that came with dealing a now single artist, producer, label owner and a definite piece of eye candy. Gerald did all he could to resist from a connection beyond business with Sandra and some days it worked and more often it didn't work. Just like a snake charmer with a whistle that could arouse and calm a venomous snake she had a voice that did that to Gerald every time she opened her mouth to sing. As a rule, he had already broken of not sleeping with anyone in the industry or partners, Sandra would be harder to break away from. For the most part Mia fell into the rule breaking as well because she was also a partner. So, with both of them he was going to have a problem trying to make a decision to break away when and if the time ever came.

Then there was the mystery lady Melanie who now was his Mel. The complete opposite of the other two, a hardworking woman who never asked or expected nothing but his company when he had time. She had a soft and caring spirit that reminded him so much of his mother and was the only one who made him totally forget about Nina whenever she was in his company without sex being involved. Out of the three clearly, she took him to heights sexually and mentally the other two hadn't come close to and with her he felt pleased it felt like time stopped as soon as her soft voice said hello, Mr. Livingston. Every moment they spent together was nothing like the previous one. Their conversations lasted for-hours, the lovemaking was beyond imagination because he truly had feelings for her, laughter that filled his penthouse and every empty dark space he tried to harbor from her. Could he settle down to a woman like her and give her what she deserved? Her past relationships ended in men cheating on her or the "it's just not working out" quote. Clearly, he was seeing other women that she knew of but never questioned his actions or whereabouts because she understood from the beginning that they were just friends and she played the part. As he laid there, he began to feel like she deserved better than that and was he the one to do it at this point in his life. Mel was in every definition of a woman, friend and possible mate…incredible. He battled with the thought could he commit and not mess it up because he couldn't be a husband. His childhood seemed to haunt him more than he cared to admit it, but he was beginning to realize that he had to deal with it one way or another and Mel told him that during one of their many conversations.

Nina honestly was an issue he hadn't dealt with, the heartbreak and the admission he was bitter. Would he ever honestly be ready to even face his part that he played in losing her? Remorse was something he never expressed about losing Nina because his anger and hurt overshadowed it. Would he be able to totally love another the way they deserved to be loved or would he just keep running? Running into a woman like Mel made him feel there was hope and or would he lose her like he lost Nina because of his failure to finally commit totally to marriage. Would he let his past continue to keep him from true love, again? Would he finally face the fact that his father whom he hadn't seen in a number of years was the reason he feared committing to Nina because of how he broke his mother's heart so bad. He gave Nina everything in the world but himself, completely but he feared one day he would hurt her just like his father hurt his mother. Nina was now married and no chance they would ever be a couple again, it was time to let her go forever. He looked up at the ceiling as the tears began to roll down the sides of his face. All the love songs he wrote, produced and sang now meant nothing to him at this moment. He sang of forever love, wrote of how to make her your lady and produced ballads for wedding songs. All his songs were geared towards love and now he was searching for the answer to the pain he felt from the pain of a love that he lost. What was he going to do now? Stop running with these three women and start over or choose one of these women in his life now. The running was getting old and fast all he wanted was companionship now but like a hairball stuck in his throat...marriage would have to at some point come to the forefront or he would be right here again.

Like clockwork Mia text a confirmation of the closing appointment for his studio and celebratory dinner reservations to follow. He confirmed still teary eyed and sat up on the side of the bed to begin to prepare mentally for their appointment. Wiping his face, he headed to the closet to pick out a suit. Tan and cream would be the colors today something about him in a suit drove Mia crazy so he knew tonight wouldn't be a night he would be returning home alone. Headed to the shower he buzzed Jay to give him a time to be ready and to confirm the location for the appointment, Jay now lived in the apartment right under his penthouse. Mia by now had helped him obtain his penthouse, a development and three business locations in addition to this latest purchase of his studio. Mia surely wasn't going to make it easy to leave her alone even with her unfinished lawful attachment and unfinished feelings she still had her husband. Shower water running he stepped in and just leaned up against the wall so the water could run down his chiseled back. Knowing all that he had on his mind all he wanted was two things, one was to hear from his mother and two was a phone call from Mel whom he really was thinking about at that moment. The shower water ran down his face blending in with his tears which still flowed from his eyes. "Oh, Nina why did you leave me? Look at this mess I have made." The words he cried out in hurt and pain as he pounded the shower wall. "Now you're gone I am alone even with these damn women" he cried out again. "God help me I am confused" he cried out as he washed himself now. Out of the shower and like a model on a page out of GQ magazine he walked out of his bedroom to the kitchen where Jay met him making jokes about how sharp dressed, he was today even caused Maria his new housekeeper to take a double look. All the way down the elevator Jay joked him about his fashion magazine look.

Mr. Sam was parked curbside as always as Jay opened the door for Gerald after removing his sport coat. It was a silent ride as Gerald looked out the window at the traffic paying more attention to the couples in cars or walking down the street. Jay put one and two together that today must be a day he was struggling with there really being no more Nina and the others must not be making the cut. Still no words exchanged thirty minutes into the ride and five minutes from the office. Mia stood curbside looking sexy as always even dressed for business. The somber face changed to a smile and ready to do business as Gerald greeted her. Gerald said,

"This shouldn't take long Jay, please let Mr. Sam know we will be dining at Sonya's Cafe afterwards."

as he walked away with Mia and Jay right behind them as usual. She almost peeled his clothes off with her eyes behind her Gucci shades and he knew it. The walk to the office was one of anticipation not for the deal to be complete but dinner and what was to happen after dinner Mia thought. While they sat at the table Mia rubbed his leg knowing exactly what side his dick laid on in his slacks when he was aroused, with a slight grin that everyone thought was because of another successful acquisition. Gerald played it cool, but he was still deep in thought as so many of them raced through his head. The check was exchanged from Gerald and the deed and keys were slid across the table. No smile but a handshake and thank you as he slid his chair back to leave with the cougar. The lender mentioned what a nice couple the two of them made and they nervously made it clear that it was strictly business. "Accept my apologies please Mr. Livingston" the lender even more nervously apologized. Gerald smiled and accepted as he exited the room. After that he really knew he needed to make some decisions with all three of them Mia, Sandra and Mel.

Once they were back in the car and the door closed Mia was all over Gerald before Jay could get in the front seat with Mr. Sam, With no fight or resistance she had her way with him right in her mouth. Gerald barely felt anything and actually all he was still thinking about was Mel. Mia enjoyed it more than he did and not wanting to mess the moment up for her, he didn't say anything but hoped the ride would be over sooner than she would be. She was so into it that she missed the fact that he was zoned out somewhere other than there with her. It was like his prayer was answered before she was able to finish him off, if it was even going to happen as the car came to a stop and Mr. Sam announced they were at the restaurant. Like clockwork she had his dick back in his slacks, zipped up, lipstick reapplied to her sexy lips and ready to exit the limo to head in for dinner. Gerald was wondering would it be a celebration dinner or just a groping session until they got back to the car and then back to his place. Gerald really wasn't mentally there but went to dinner anyway staying far enough away that she couldn't touch anything but his hands on the table while they talked before the food came to the table. Ordering dinner was simple, two grilled chicken salads and a bottle of champagne.

Mia was always excited whenever Gerald closed on a property because she thought it made him happy and she got a hefty kickback as well. Tonight, was different for Gerald more than likely because of the moment of reality he had before he met up with Mia and finally, she could see it in his face. Doing everything she could not to agitate whatever the situation that may have been troubling him at least while they were at dinner, so she kept small talk at the table. Dinner didn't last long and actually was cut short by Gerald but not to rush Mia to his place and satisfy her aching need for him but to drop her off at her place and he headed home heavy on the mind and heart. Mia was disappointed but understood and let him know she was just a phone call away. He knew this way of life wasn't what he wanted and not pleasing to his mother whom he knew was looking down on him in complete disappointment with his activities with these three women. All the way home he looked out the window at the now dim lit sky as the streetlights began to come on and people were beginning to come out to walk and exercise. Jay knew his cousin was deep in thought and just left him alone.

They pulled up in front of the building and Gerald exited the car before Jay could even open the door for him. Gerald never looked back at Mr. Sam as he walked to the front door with his head down and his hands in his pockets. The elevator ride was a quiet one much different from earlier when Jay was joking him about his magazine fashion attire. As they exited the elevator Gerald let Jay know he would be staying in for the night and if he wanted to, he could knock off early. Jay continued to follow as if Gerald never even said anything in the hallway, securing Gerald and checked Maria's sexy body out as usual. Gerald requested a glass of his favorite wine on his way back to his room. Maria fixed his glass of wine and pulled out an empty glass unsure if he had any company coming over. Jay stopped her with a head nod to let her know there would be no one else tonight. Gerald was undressed and back where he started earlier in the day with nothing, but candles lit so the darkness would hide the tears that were streaming down his face. Maria placed the tray on the footstool and made sure he was ok and if he would need anything else, he told her he wouldn't need anything else and relieved her for the night as well.

He laid there and just questioned himself...What was he going to do? A man who had everything and could get anything he wanted felt like he had nothing right now. Would he keep running or stop and face what he was running from, himself and his past.

CHAPTER 5

"The Phone Call"

THE SUN HAD BEGUN TO break through the morning darkness. He had been there in Atlanta a little over six months and was getting comfortable in his new place, but he still hadn't picked up a pen, turned on his iPad or Mac to do anything with his own music. He was still dating; wining and dining three beautiful Georgia peaches life was back to the "G" he was before Nina. The emotional rollercoaster was still in motion, some days he was happy or so it seemed, but it was evident he was definitely trying to fill a void. He had been thinking heavily for the past few days about this fresh start that now was clouded because of his own actions. He laid there and looked up at the ceiling which was his favorite place to think as the tears began to stream down the sides of his face, things had gotten to a point, he couldn't even hear himself pray and wondered if his prayers were even being heard.

Like clockwork six thirty his phone lit up with his morning text from Mel. He leaned over with a slight smile on face until he saw...Nina's name in front of the text. His heart raced and almost paralyzed his hand making him drop the phone on the bed, rubbing his head down over his face,

"What the fuck? Why? What could she possibly want?"

he let out in a fury of anger. As he was about swipe to open Nina's text another text came through that was Mel's text which quickly changed his fury to his morning smile whenever she would text him and opened the text to,

"Good morning Sir today will be better than yesterday. I will see you curbside at 4:05 prompt. I cannot wait to see you baby."

Almost forgetting their date he responded,

"You have no clue how much I needed your text this morning, Mel. I cannot wait to see you too baby."

During their texting exchange he was questioning what Nina could want after over a year of no calls, text or phone call since she left him. After laying there thinking about just deleting the text but anticipation killed that idea, so he clicked on the text that simply said,

"Gerald, I am sure you are mad at me but, can we please talk?"

A sigh of frustration escaped his lungs, and he typed his reply,

"About what Nina? I think you said all you wanted and needed to say when you left me with a letter and clearly you showed me when you got married not much longer after doing that."

He threw the phone on the bed and got up slipped his slippers on made his way to the bathroom while clicking the remote to open the electric blinds to let the sun in and turned on some music as he always did to start his day. The penthouse had become his personal toy chest that he equipped with every type of gadget available he could be quite a big kid as he bounced in and out of the bathroom to make the motion sensor lights go on and off. Morning ritual of magazine in hand and the news on the tv in the bathroom. He read one article then he shaved his head and clicked the remote for the shower to come on all six heads came on full stream as he entered. The water fired from all of the jets hitting him front and back until he sat down and just let the water and steam relax him. After about ten minutes he showered and made his way out to dry off over the sink looking in the mirror as the steam was sucked up in the ceiling, he wondered what Nina could possibly have to say after all this time. He finished in the bathroom and got himself ready for an eight o'clock investment meeting and had some breakfast. Dressed and ready waiting for Mr. Sam to arrive he grabbed another glass of orange juice. The door opened and the phone rang at the same time as Maria entered,

"Mr. Gerald, Mr. Sam is parked out front waiting."

Sucking down his juice making his way to the door Maria stood there with his briefcase,

"Have a good day Mr. Gerald."

Three steps to the elevator opened to the six-foot eleven massive machine without a smile, Jay.

"Good morning Mr. Gerald."

once the doors closed Jay chuckled and made notice this was the first morning in a while Gerald was leaving alone or didn't have one of the ladies leave out before him. They both chuckled and back to straight faces as the elevator neared the lobby. Gerald grabbed another paper as they left the lobby leaving his normal ten dollars for a two-dollar newspaper. Making his way past the front desk and almost pass the concierge who rushed to open the door to the sunny warm weather striking up some small talk in hopes of a healthy tip as he heard from others Mr. Gerald was known for giving. Almost breaking his leg to get to the car door only to be blocked by Jay's huge arm. Gerald reached around Jay and handed him a tip with a word,

"You had the tip at the front door son, calm down no amount of money is worth embarrassing yourself or running into a brick wall like Jay."

while slipping into the shiny black limo as the door closed to hide him and his troubled mind behind the dark windows.

Always a giving person before but since his heartbreak he became much humbler and more compassionate to others. As the car neared the corner, he lowered his window to give the homeless gentleman his daily ten dollars and wished him a good day. As he raised his window the phone rang, it was like he saw a ghost when he looked at the screen like it was six thirty a.m. again and Jay saw it all over his face,

"G what is wrong? Who is it?"

Jay lifted up to the edge of seat to question Gerald while almost taking the phone from him until Gerald showed him the screen that displayed Nina's name and picture which shockingly was still saved in his phone. Remembering her mild persistence when she wanted his attention or a response, he answered her call instead of neglecting it. A reluctant greeting, he gave only to hear,

"Gerald... (a long pause followed) I need to talk to you and the first thing I want to say is I am sorry; I am so sorry. I don't know what I was thinking if I was thinking at all. (She could hear him breathing heavy) Before you hang up on me or even let me have it just know that there's not a day that goes by that I don't think of you. Gerald I am so sorry."

In total shock and lost for words or a response fitting to what she said to him all Gerald could say was,

"You were my world and when you left you took it with you Nina. Now that I have begun to put the pieces together that I can or at least buy to put something new together and now you are calling me to say what? I tell you what, to make ease of what you did which you know was selfish and fucked up because you wanted what you wanted when you wanted it!"

Then dead silence remained for about two minutes. On both ends of the phone tears rolled down both of their faces only Jay was there for Gerald and Nina was alone in her office finally she blurted out,

"Gerald...Gerald...I will be in Atlanta for a seminar in two weeks and I would really like to sit down and talk with you. It is so much I want to say that I don't want to say over the phone. Please Gerald, please?"

Like a loaded gun he fired right back,

"You see what I mean, it's what you need, what you want but what about me? Nina, I don't know I have to think about it. I am at my destination and I need to get myself together before I go in here to this meeting. I am not hanging up on you, but I am saying goodbye Nina. I will let you know before it is time for you to come to Atlanta."

as he ended the call. He now rode in silence and Jay gave him a few minutes before he checked on him and to ask if his meeting should be cancelled. Gerald insisted the show go on and requested that nothing else be said about her or the conversation.

Meanwhile back in Chicago Nina was crying her eyes out locked in her office filled with some of the same mixed emotions that Gerald was feeling in Atlanta as the tears rolled down his face. A portion of the emotions was happiness because Gerald answered the phone, a portion was hurt because he was so abrasive and didn't even remember this was the day, they met and angry because she felt like he didn't make mention of his part that he played in all of this to make her feel like it was best for her to leave. Ten years and no marriage or even a child, she looked around her office and all she saw was Gerald today, from the custom built mahogany desk to the matching mahogany meeting table that they made love on, on numerous occasions, the flowers he set up to be delivered every Monday morning as long as she was in that office that he never discontinued and she didn't decline when they were delivered every Monday, the rug under her desk because he had her rubbing her feet on the carpet like he would do when he took his shoes off and all the mahogany matching lamp tables he ordered while she was on a trip and had the rest of her office set up. As the tears continued to roll down her face she wondered if calling was even the right thing to do, would she hear from him again or would he even answer when she called him back.

CHAPTER 6

"Addressing the Hurt"

IT WAS DATE NIGHT AND Mia felt separated from Gerald, confused and very unfamiliar with the feeling and reactions that Gerald was giving off. She did all she could to figure out an approach to get him to talk about Nina and the phone call because it was apparent that it was bothering him as they walked around Lenox Mall.

"Gerald, you seem like you are somewhere else tonight, so far away. I am very familiar with how you are feeling at this stage in life because of where I am in my own life with my situation, but the difference is, I am married, and you weren't. Maybe you should try to talk to her and bring closure to that part of your life. I say that as your lover and more importantly as your friend. You are a wonderful man and you have made a positive stride to move forward but you will not be totally happy because you haven't closed that chapter of you and Nina and whether it is with me or someone else you will keep coming to this point. I care a great deal about you, and I want the best for you, but you have to address this"

Mia firmly said to Gerald as she stopped grabbing both of his hands while looking up at him in his eyes. With every word she spoke Gerald's eyes glazed and he grabbed her hand tighter as they continued to walk through the mall. Mia laid her head on Gerald's shoulder knowing Gerald needed her more tonight than any other night. The stares and occasional stops to sign autographs didn't even phase him but it was surely irritating Jay.

Although her words weren't what he wanted to hear he listened and digested them as well. Mia knew what he was feeling and gripped his hand just as tight as he squeezed her hand. They walked in silence did some more shopping and headed back to his place afterwards. The ride home was in silence as they continued to hold hands and Mia laid on Gerald's shoulder kissing his hand every so often. They pulled up to the curb the doorman came out to help with the bags as Gerald and Mia exited to the lobby door

Jay of course right behind him asked if he would need him anymore for the evening and if not, he would let Mr. Sam know he was done for the evening as well. Gerald looked at Mia as he nodded no. They walked into the building straight to the waiting elevator, Jay walked the two to the door, made sure the bags made their way up as well and let Gerald know he would be down in the lounge for a while if he needed him. Jay was familiar with this feeling that he was getting from Gerald and knew he would need to stick close by. Mia whispered to Jay she would take care of Gerald for the rest of the evening. Maria was still there almost done cooking dinner and prepared to leave once it was finished and served. She knew of his women activities and sometimes would joke with him about it and would ask, "who am I cooking for tonight?" but knew tonight wasn't one of those nights by the look on his face and the somber greeting he gave as he went straight back to his room. Mia was informed of the baked salmon, mashed potatoes, garlic seasoned asparagus and his favorite red velvet cake was in the cake dish. Maria told Mia she would let herself out and would be back in the morning in time to have breakfast prepared for them.

Gerald had undressed and got in the shower just standing there letting the water run down his back with his against the wall. Mia lit a few candles they brought while in the mall and dimmed the bedroom lights. The sound of some soft music playing, and the aroma of eucalyptus should help to relax him she thought. Unsure if company in the shower would add to his confused mind she just waited on the sofa in his bedroom until he called out to her,

"Mia, can you bring me a towel and wash my back please?"

Mia undressed out of her sundress and his favorite Victoria Secret lace boy shorts and bra set grabbed a fresh towel and made her way into the bathroom where her heart began pumping a double dose of blood flow as the anticipation built for what was about to happen in the shower or so she hoped was about to happen. He opened the shower door for her to enter and sat down on the bench with his legs open for her to see his now hardening manhood while motioning her to come closer. He reached for her soft hips that tried to hide her phat ass that he loved. Pulling her into hug her while resting his head on her flat stomach right underneath her beautiful firm breast. She did all she could to just hold him close, but her hands began to rub his sculpted shoulders, arms and back. Her legs inside of his felt his dick pressed between them now and they stayed like that for about five minutes until she reached for the soap and washcloth only to be stopped by his hands pulling her in for a kiss. Her heart was racing, and she tried so hard to stay focused on washing his back only to be lifted off of her feet and pressed against the shower wall while he kissed her on her neck breathing heavily in her ear as he lifted one leg placed it on his hip and rubbed her now throbbing pussy with the other hand. The passion from his kisses and now hands all over her body he knew would have the honey in her pot ready to be stirred. He pulled her closer and slid inside of her all at one time. No matter how many times they had been together he knew she had to adjust to him, and he let her as he slowly worked himself in and out of her until she had it all inside of her. The soft moans and whispering of his name, "Gerald, Gerald... Gerald", with her nails lightly digging in his back let him know she was receiving him, all of him. Slowly he made love to her mind, body and soul. The kisses became more intense and her moans drove him crazy as his hands grabbed and gripped her ass, he was relentless until she climaxed holding him so he could not move as she breathed heavily while lightly biting on his shoulder. The hot water just ran over their bodies until Mia's body relaxed and he sat back down on the bench for Mia to back up to him and have a seat back on him as she slid him back inside of her, he rubbed her back making her jerk and moan every time he got to the small of her back, she would arch with her ass pushed back on him and chest pushed forward which caused the tightness of pussy to rub against the vein of his dick just right making him lose it in return. Rubbing and smacking her ass softly as she rode him like a smooth, well trained horse rider not too long into that position the sounds of her climaxing filled the shower walls loudly. He picked her up and put her back up against the wall with her legs locked in the creases of his arms and worked her over like a trainer in the gym. The tables were now turned as he moaned her name as she looked him in his eyes telling him,

"It's yours fill it up with your warm cum baby, please I needed you so bad. Why do you make me wait so long Gerald?"

To silence her talking to just a moan he went deeper inside of her and not to long after he filled her with what she asked for and kept going until she climaxed again shortly after. Kissing and holding each other as he lowered her down, they kissed more up against the shower wall as the water poured down on them. Finally, they walked back over to the bench and sat down holding hands and she layed her head on his shoulder for a few minutes Gerald said with a bit of sarcasm,

"I guess I need more than my back washed now."

Making love in the shower was something they loved to do, and Mia was worn out this time as they washed each other Mia was hoping he wouldn't want another round. The water began to finally cool as they finished showering. There was only one towel available, so he told her to dry off as he stood there and watched her dry off enjoying the site while self-consciously questioning himself. What is really going to come from this? What if Mel catches feelings and wants more than they have established in such a short time? The questions ended fast when Mia came back in with a towel to dry him off. Wrapped in her towel still hoping he wouldn't want a round two because she was still tingling inside from round one and she felt him looking at her every move from the mirror and eye to eye whenever she would look at him. To distract him she kept some small conversation about a movie in bed after the delicious meal Maria had prepared. Just like any man all he heard was food and responded,

"Do you mind fixing our plates and I will grab the dinner trays for us"

as he patted her on her ass as she walked away. She figured no need to put anything on he was just going to take it off anyway, so she just walked around in her towel.

Like a kid prepared for one of his favorite meals that Maria cooked Gerald sat there on the edge of the Italian imported cream leather sofa ready to attack the defenseless plate of food he waited for her with the dinner tables all set up. As she placed the plates of food on their tables and grabbed them some wine to go with their food, he listened to Anita Baker sing, "Angel." She came back with the bottle and two wine glasses he watched her get them ready then they prayed over the food and began to eat. After a few minutes of silence because Gerald was ripping through his food he finally spoke,

"You know what hurt me the most? Not the fact that she left but how she did it and to add injury to insult the mere feeling that this man she married not even a year later was someone she had been seeing or talking to for some time."

Mia made sure he had finished before she expressed how she understood how she felt because her husband had left her with no notice at all and popped up with a three-month pregnant girlfriend which was both embarrassing and painful. She then asked,

"Gerald be honest with yourself first and then with everybody else did she give you any indications at all she was either unhappy or she was planning on leaving or wanted more and you just missed it? Or chose to ignore it? I am not taking her side at all so please don't get defensive with me. Did you do anything to make her feel that leaving was the only or best solution?"

His only response after thinking for a minute or two was,

"She kept saying all these years and a beautiful ring when I question you about us getting married, that's all? I hope you will make us official" after a short pause he then mumbled, "I guess I was so caught up with my career that the seriousness of marriage was ignored, and I thought her smile was genuine. Which makes it hurt even more. I may have missed the mark, but she was wrong for how she left!"

Mia responded cautiously but sincerely,

"Which is all the more reason you need to speak to her to close the door to what you feel and don't have the answers to, Gerald. I really want you to take an honest and deep moment and think about the part you played in her making the decisions she made to leave and not leave but to marry the first man that she dated. You owe all of this to yourself and whoever you decide to make your next woman in your life."

He had no response after she said what she said so he just ate his dinner and occasionally gazed out the window in between each forkful of food.

The rest of the meal was pretty much quiet until Gerald apologized for anything that he may have said that may have hurt Mia's feelings unlike ninety percent of the time since they had been seeing each other she was the aggressor in their conversations and would have been the first to say something, but this time given the touchy subject she didn't. Sliding her tray to the side and getting up to move his as well she pulled his head in to place it on her stomach while rubbing his bald head then she pulled him up to lead him over to the king size platform bed. Both of their towels fell to the floor as they walked over to the bed, she placed a soft kiss on his lips before they laid on the bed with her laid up on his chest as he held her then she whispered,

"I really just want to lay here and listen to you whether it is your words or just your heart beating because I genuinely care about you Gerald. No matter how this turns out I want to be friends first."

The night sky had fallen over Atlanta and they laid there with her in his arms looking out the window at the sky and stars in silence until she dozed off and he held her closer while thinking about all that Mia said and the phone call from Nina.

Here he was laying with a woman any man would love to have in his life but the one who left her evidently. Then there was Mel who clearly worshipped the ground that he walked on and was about to walk on even with the uncertainty of what their future would bring. Sandra, the no pressure lover who all she really wanted was a record deal in the beginning but has become even more of a friend as well. All three of these women accepted that he was not ready for a commitment at all and accepted that he was seeing other women, right now. All three of them had careers of their own and ran a close race of pleasing his every need both mentally and physically. It was obvious that he was still painfully in love with the one who broke his heart into a million tiny pieces and struggled with the idea that none of them were Nina. He questioned himself and wondered if his life-long hurt of seeing how the relationship between his parents was a part of the reason he was unable to make or even the thought of actually committing to a wedding date. Nina was everything in a woman he could ever imagine and more but, it took for her to leave a letter, the ring and everything he had ever given her to see how much she really meant to him and his mere squeaky clean professional and personal existence was because of their relationship. Gerald was angry about her leaving the way she did and the length of time that had passed before any contact at all only to see it in a newspaper and all over the television that the long-time woman in Gerald's life had been seeing someone else and shortly after that a wedding date had been announced. He had everything physically but without her in his life right now it was just, things.

Mia nestled closer and Gerald looked down at her sleeping while rubbing her now short curly hair. He whispered,

"I feel so secure with you Mia...I really do."

He kissed her on the forehead as he closed his eyes till, he dozed off. Still troubled, even if he was to decide to make a go with Mia she was still married and wasn't ready for anything serious and she made it clear at times when she would say that they were good at business together and good friends. Which is also a part of what landed him in the bed with three different women now and has made way for a circle of mixed feelings since his phone call from the woman he truly ever loved outside of his Mom. He still loved her but still held onto the hurt from how she left him, she is now married and now wanting to do what she did in the place of a letter, have a face-to-face conversation. What is it that she could possibly have to say, what could he say in response to whatever she had to say? Mia planted something in his mind and on his heart tonight that sparked a flame for him to think about his part he played in the decision for her to just up and leave.

Flashbacks of his parents and their failed relationship constantly played on his decision of when and if he would marry or not. His mom was a beautiful schoolteacher who worshipped the ground that his father walked on until Gerald's eleventh birthday when they walked into the grocery store on Eighth Street to grab some things for his birthday party only to see his father walking with a woman and playing with a boy who looked just like him and about the same age as he was that he found out later was his half-brother who was just a month younger than him. The lady he saw his father with was another teacher that worked at the same school that his mom had been transferred from right after she found she was pregnant with Gerald. He could still hear his Mom explaining that she was being transferred to another school and wouldn't be able to walk him to school on her way to her school as a result of the transfer. Gerald never spoke to his father again until his mother's funeral on his thirty-first birthday. Their birthdays were exactly seven days apart which helped to further explain the tight bond that they shared. Seeing his Father for the first time in twenty years didn't go to well not only had he lost his mom, his rock and best friend that he was sure died from a broken heart. Ms. Mona as everyone called her passed away suddenly on her fifty-third birthday as Gerald walked across the stage to receive his first Grammy.

Gerald feared he would become the monster that he called his father and he too would be the reason some beautiful women would suffer from a broken heart just like his mother. What he feared most turned around on him as far as the broken heart because of his fear of being just like his father the monster as he called him, and he was the one to be hurt because of his fear of being like his father. Chris and Jay were the only ones who knew the depth of the hurt Gerald carried because of how his is Father hurt his Mom and fully understood why Nina leaving affected him like it did. When Nina came into his life Gerald was a lady's man, but he knew in order to meet and court her he had to change his lifestyle and the playboy status had to be retired. He always prided her for coming along just before the man whom he never wanted to become took over his life.

Given the short amount time he had known these three women and the circumstances under how he met them with the exception of Sandra who he had known for some time before his move to Atlanta. Gerald felt that out of all three of these women he was involved with, Mia had the potential to help him out of this hidden web of hurt whether they were to pursue a relationship or remain just friends. Both Jay and Chris were secretly rooting for Mia based on all of the in-depth conversations they shared but Mel was in a close running as well more so because she comes with no baggage. Which made the thought of Gerald ever securing a lifetime mate again very difficult because he struggled with the question if either of them had the potential to replace Nina. Jay repeatedly told him stop looking for someone to replace Nina and open yourself up to who and what you have in front of you, if it is meant to be it will be and not a moment before. Chris kept telling him to slow down and take his time with all of them because,

...hurt can hurt even more when it is compounded with yet another hurt, take time to heal first. Words Chris told Gerald over and over again. He said it so much the words were imbedded in his memory.

He always said it was a fresh start but the move seemed more like a way to get away from the possible intensified hurt he feared of seeing Nina with her now husband in person and the looks that people would give when they saw him in public without her. Was this the move to make toyed around in his mind along with doubt even after he now had settled into a life in Atlanta. So, use to everything having a price on it to bring happiness he was seeing that only covered the hurt and the involvement of these women in a way were clouding his move but, in a way, they gave him hope that there was a chance that he could bounce back and recover from the hurt of losing Nina. He begun to come to realization that he had to address the hurt from his Father's actions.

CHAPTER 7

"At the Crossroad"

MIA'S ALARM SOUNDED AT FIVE thirty as it did every morning for her early workout session. Gerald was sound asleep, so she eased out of the bed showered and dressed quietly careful not to wake him knowing he had a rough time going to sleep last night. She jotted down a short note letting him know she didn't want to wake him and would talk to him later. As she exited the bedroom and down the hall, she could smell a fresh pot of coffee brewing and Maria cooking breakfast. Maria insisted she at least take a bottle of orange juice before she left. Mia took the orange juice and bottle of water before she left and wished Maria a wonderful day in Maria's native tongue of Spanish leaving her with a smile. Jay was on the elevator headed down for his workout as well. Jay not being a morning person submitted a grumpy good morning as he stepped aside to let her in the elevator while taking her bags from the day of shopping they did yesterday. The ride down was quiet just the sounds of pecks on their phones checking their schedules for the day. As the elevator came to the lobby floor the doors opened to of course the anxious concierge in hopes that it was Mr. G as they called him now. Jay interrupted quite irritated and ordered transportation for Mia to get home. Slipping him a tip and telling Mia he would see her later and to have a good day. The front desk attendant dazed at the site of Mia in her yoga pants he fumbled with greeting her and Jay quickly corrected him and assisted him to regain focus,

"Good morning Mam would be the appropriate thing to say since your mouth is already open my friend."

With a chuckle behind her smile on her face Mia thanked Jay, he offered a workout in the gym with him, but she let him know she was going to her gym then home to get dressed for work as they walked out to get in her car service. He saw to her and her bags were safely into the car and gave a thumbs up as he walked back into the building.

Al Johnson

The aroma from Maria's breakfast cooking nor Mel's good morning text didn't even wake Gerald this morning. Maria closed his door and began her daily chores in the already spotless penthouse. The morning sun began to peek in and finally woke Gerald as he rolled over feeling for Mia only to find she was already gone. He then rolled back over on his back and looked up at the ceiling. His mind wondered what would happen this morning especially after the morning he had yesterday. The smell of breakfast was in the air and he called for Maria to bring him his plate which was even weird even to her because his ritual was to read the paper then shower and watch the news at the breakfast bar. Maria acknowledged she heard him, "Be right there Mr. G" as she prepared his plate. Gerald laid there a little longer feeling disappointed that Mia had left without waking him up and finally he rolled over, got up to brush his teeth that's when he found the note, she left folded over on the nightstand on his side of the bed that she left with a kiss with red lipstick. Immediately his heart rate began to increase because it was like a flashback of Nina's exit letter. Hesitant to read it he left it there and went to brush his teeth wondering if it was something, he said to cause her to just leave a note and not wake him up. He didn't turn the tv on or pick up his morning paper that Maria left for him as soon as she would come in for work, he just stood in front of the mirror and stared until his vision went blurry.

"Mr. Gerald your breakfast, juice and coffee are on the table will you be needing anything else right now?"

Maria said as she picked up his clothes off the floor. A soft response filled with confusion,

"No Maria not right now."

Making sure the door was closed as he came out the bathroom and as he walked over to get the note his reminder of the morning text from Mel sounded. Almost as if the sun shined and the rain fell at the same time as he grabbed the note and his phone at the same time. Responding to Mel in one hand and opening the note in other one, a sigh of relief was released as he read the note from Mia. Relieved after he read the note, he then sent a good morning text to Mia. Taking a seat on the sofa turning on the tv and opening the blinds to let some sun in while he ate his breakfast. The sun lit up his room and his eyes as well as he opened his emails.

The smell of Mia was still in the blanket on the sofa which gave him a pleasant thought as her response came through,

58

"Still at the gym baby. Will call you after I shower and on my way to my first appointment." Almost forgetting to check Mel's response still feeling a sigh of relief that nothing was wrong with Mia as a result of the conversation that they had last night. Maria announced Jay was coming in as if the sound of his big feet in his size fourteen shoes walking across the marble floors would require him to need one. Jay came in with a bagel that looked like it disappeared in his huge hand. He sat down next to Gerald asking about the plans for the day while having some small talk. Jay watched Gerald get back into his routine and it brought a smile to his face seeing him multitask looking over some paperwork, phone next to him and eating his breakfast.

"What are you smiling about Jay?"

Jay responded,

"Either Mia left you happy or you are fully coming around my brother."

Gerald smiled and responded,

"A little of both, I need to figure out some things Jay, but I also need to get back into the swing of things with my own music too, but business has to go on until I can get back into it in the meantime. Can you have Mr. Sam and the car ready by eleven? I am going to see Mel for lunch then I have a meeting in Smyrna with Sandra at three-thirty to go over some music. We will be done by seven at the latest."

Jay was waiting to hear if it was going to be Mel or Mia for the nights company, but nothing was mentioned so he left to give Mr. Sam notice of his needed arrival time. Gerald text Mel that he would see her shortly then continued to answer a few emails while he finished his breakfast and turned on some Jill Scott to give his morning a jumpstart while preparing for the day ahead. He then made his way to the bathroom where the music played from the speakers in the ceiling and with the click of a switch the shower came on and he danced his way into the shower letting the water hit his head and back the jets were set on massage. After his fifteen-minute shower he exited and brushed his teeth again and walked out to an already made bed and plate removed out of the room. He walked into his perfectly organized closet selecting a gray Armani two-piece suit, white tailored shirt and a pair of black Ferragamo shoes. He stood in the middle of his closet thinking about the phone call from Nina, the conversation with Mia, Mel's smile and her willingness to cater to his every need and the mystery woman Sandra whom he knew was ready at any time he was ready to make the next move.

Even with all the pros of all three of these beautiful women he still struggled with deep confused feelings for Nina and no matter how mad and hurt he was, he had to admit he was curious what she could possibly have to say and how she had the nerve to even call him almost insisting that they sit down and talk. Should he entertain her or do her like she did him by leaving a note on the table wherever they are supposed to meet but knowing that was not his style the thought of doing that was quickly dismissed. Mia was a close match to all of what Nina was, but he just kept coming back to her having unfinished business with her should be soon to be ex-husband. Mel was just innocent and gradually falling in love with him or was it the infatuation of all the sex and lavish outings that he showered her with or was it he was starting to fall for her and didn't want to admit it. Daydreaming into all these repeated thoughts until Maria knocked on the door startling him,

"Mr. Gerald, are you ready? Mr. Sam will be here in fifteen minutes and Jay is waiting in the kitchen for you. Your briefcase and umbrella are in the kitchen next to the island. If there won't be anything else, I will return to prepare your dinner after I run some errands and stop at the market then to pick up some fresh flowers for the table at the front door?"

Gerald let her know he would be home around eight and to prepare something special for dinner for two.

Looking like a sex symbol out of a magazine again today as he slipped his suit jacket on as he walked out of his bedroom down the hall stopping to pick up his briefcase and umbrella. Jay could see the look of deep thought on his boss and cousin face as he took his things as they walked out the door to hop on the elevator. The elevator ride down was silent until Gerald asked Jay,

"What am I doing? Nina has called and I have no clue what to do about this requested meet and talk. Mia is just remarkable but somewhat tarnished by her situation. Then there is Mel, well I must admit she is my little joy and getaway from everything because of her youth and no real problems or obstacles that I can see thus far. Sandra as he paused for a minute is like bait hanging out for this shark to jump out of the water and get her. I have relocated and bounced back into my old way of living before Nina, just here in Atlanta now. I still have my condo in Chicago I haven't been able to move a thing out of or around in over a year. I am living a life anyone would love to live but I am ripped to shreds on the inside. My heart is still in some fucked up kind of way with Nina and hers is encased in a wedding ring married to another man. What do I do?" As the elevator doors opened Jay could only respond,

"You definitely have to let go of Nina and realize that she is gone, there is nothing that can bring that situation back to you and even if it were to end with her husband all you would remember is how she left the first time. Can you honestly answer yes, to the question if she was to come back that you would be able to forgive her and not live with any doubts that she would do it again if you didn't move on something else, she wanted? I want you to really think about your part you also played in the demise and eventually making Nina leave you. That is the harsh reality from my heart G. These other women you are mingling with may not even be the women meant to fill the empty space in your heart that Nina has left you with G."

Gerald wasn't expecting that response especially after hearing the same question from Mia last night about his part he played or may have played that made Nina leave him. Gerald looked stunned as he exited behind Jay as he switched to his business face and greeted folks in the lobby signed a few autographs and made his way to the limo greeting Mr. Sam. The business face changed once he was in the back seat. Now that he was behind the dark windows his face expressed how he really felt, confused and troubled. Jay transitioned to the business for the day to take Gerald's mind off what he knew would soon bring him to a crossroad and force to him to make some life decisions.

CHAPTER 8

"What Do You Want from Me?"

THE DOWNTOWN ATLANTA TRAFFIC MADE the already stiff atmosphere in the car even tighter giving Gerald more time to think about what Mia and Jay had to say which made the ride seem that much longer with all the stop and go traffic. Jay ran out of positive things to say and all the business on the agenda for the rest of the week had been discussed. Jay was saved by the bell when Mia called to tell Gerald another property was acquired and there was a potential buyer for it already once the renovations were completed. Some naughty talk was exchanged and just like that Gerald was smiling again. Mr. Sam lowered the partition to let them know they were five minutes from the first stop which was to take to Mel for lunch. Gerald ended the call with Mia with a smile and a thank you. As they arrived Mel stood by the curb dressed in a sexy red sundress displaying her every curve as she proceeded to the car with a big smile on her face only to be stopped by the doorman so he could open the car door hoping to get a glimpse of the new mystery man who has put a glow on her face and a new pep in her step. Jay got out to block that from happening and assisted her into the car making his way up to the front of the car afterwards with Mr. Sam who then pulled away fast headed to their lunch destination, The Optimist was a café where they were having lunch and Gerald was a silent partner now. She was unable to say anything to her lunch date because he was on the phone the entire ride, so she just sat across from him looking at him like he was her appetizer not on the menu before lunch. The ride wasn't long, and his call ended just as Mr. Sam pulled up in front of the restaurant. While waiting to be taken inside Gerald looked at her like an inspector of fine art making her blush as she said,

"Well, hello my baby."

Jay walked in to do a quick look around and make sure the arrangements were completed for a secluded seating for Gerald and Mel. Jay came back out and escorted them in swiftly as only he knew how to do from all the years, he had protected Gerald and then Nina. Mel was in between learning how to move as well and surely spoiled by all the eyes and attention by not only the lookers but Jay too who seemed to have taken a liking to the one, he called the short cutie with the Georgia Peach Booty only to Gerald. After they were seated, and safety was insured Jay took his place at the front door every so often sticking his head in to check on Gerald and Mel.

Now that the pre-entrance had been completed Gerald waited for his proper greeting exchange of hello baby and a kiss since he missed it because he was on the phone. The owner and now partner sent a bottle of house Merlot to the table. Two chicken salads arrived promptly to the table which had to be strategically placed not to interrupt the two love birds as they engaged in some kissing and long stirs into each other eyes. Mel's glow on her face and her conversation today was different from the past three months. Her innocent beauty and attentiveness were all that Gerald needed and wanted right there at that moment. They attempted to eat but there was something different today between the two of them and Gerald could feel but unlike any other time he would try to distract it with a joke or some conversation to change the mood but this time he actually relaxed and let it happen. They just sat there holding hands and kissing like two in love teenagers. Not much of the salads were eaten and the bottle of wine looked untouched minus their two pours as it still sat on the table. The waiter just stood off to the side until they were ready for something else before going back to the table.

An hour went by all of her lipstick was gone and they never lost eye contact. It was clear from the mutual body language that Mel would be his company for the night. The patiently waiting waiter finally interrupted,

"Will there be take home containers for anything today, Sir?"

The owner stepped in and gestured the waiter to remove the dishes fully aware of the time frame they had for lunch. Jay walked over to remind Gerald of his next appointment. Mel had a face of disappointment only to be told she would be spending the rest of the day with him. As the café' began to fill the owner arranged for them to exit through the rear exit where the car was now waiting for them. Mr. Sam was prepared to head back to the Westin until Gerald instructed him that Mel would be staying with him the rest of the day. Jay displayed that devilish grin again as the privacy window went back up, of all three Mel was the one he secretly liked the most for Gerald. The kissing and holding hands in the café' continued in the car with limits or at least they attempted to keep it within limits because of his appointment. The kissing was intense again and Mel was all over him finally she came up for air as she rubbed Gerald's bald head down to his groomed beard looking into his eyes almost lost for words, she was able to ask,

"How long is this Heaven with you going to last?"

Before he could respond she put her finger over his mouth followed by another kiss. The congested traffic made it that much more difficult for them to stop peeling each other's clothes off especially after he went up under her sundress only to find she wasn't wearing anything at all. He ran his long thick fingers over her short, groomed hair honey pot down to her already wet spot. Teasing her with a few rubs between her phat pussy lips up to her clit as soft moans escaped her mouth. He pulled her closer as he kissed her to quiet the moans, he could feel her heart racing behind her full breast with his other hand as he cupped them. She laid her head back against the seat and sighed as she gasped and climaxed from him rubbing her now swollen clit in a circular motion.

Jay buzzed his phone to let him know they were ten minutes away from his appointment with Sandra. Mel helped him straighten his clothes as they both chuckled like two teenage kids sneaking in the backseat of their parent's car.

"G we have arrived. Be right there it is beginning to rain?"

Gerald tried to decline Jay's assistance, but Jay was at the door like he never declined. They got one more kiss till he would return back to her. Jay cleared his throat as he stood there at the door with his umbrella and Gerald exited while instructing Mr. Sam to take Mel to the mall and let her do a little shopping for about two hours. Like always he attempted to give her some money to go shopping but she declined it as always.

"I will be here for at least two hours baby then we will head back to the house." Gerald whispered to Mel while Jay was on the phone calling inside to let them know they were downstairs as they headed inside Gerald looked back at the car pulling off. Mel put the window down and waved back at him like a kid about to go to the toy store. Once Gerald and Jay walked in Sandra was walking out of the elevator greeting him with a big smile and a hug all in the same breath, she started telling him about all the music she had written and the beats that had been done. Gerald was thinking about Mel, so he just nodded his head and took at her book of lyrics to look over them as they entered the elevator. Jay knowing Gerald as well as he did, he gave him a light pinch on his side to snap him out of his deep thought. Once they exited the elevator to the studio the sound of the music brought him back to his world that he knew so well.

"Gerald, I see something caught your eye the way you are bobbing your head that is all my work."

Sandra said proudly. The booth was ready and his once keyboard man Keith, was at the boards with a smile. Greeted by a handshake and a hug Gerald immediately was ready to get to work.

Sandra grabbed a bottle of water and walked into the booth covering about seven tracks for Gerald. Each track was better than the last one. The last track titled, "Waiting on You" that Sandra poured her heart into and Gerald knew that one was meant for him and it was a sure hit. The hook was,

"You could design my heart out of clay as if you were a master potter and it would beat when you breathed life into it."

Jay's eyebrow even raised feeling it as well. The session was over four hours later which was well past the two-hour time frame he gave Mel and Sandra surely sealed her record deal. She was a dangling fish just as Gerald said and he was the shark. A reminder text was quickly sent to remind Gerald that Mel was out in the car and had been there for a few minutes. Which meant she must have had a good shopping session and wouldn't be upset for the extra two hours he had been in the studio.

Gerald gave a verbal yes and head nod to Jay was exchanged as a meeting to be scheduled to go over some contracts to sign Sandra for her next four CDs was given. Sandra hugged and thanked him for about three minutes until Jay pinched him on his side again so that Gerald would get out of there without dropping the hook and make another situation for himself tonight. As smoothly as Jay ushered him into the café', he did the same thing getting him out of the studio. As they walked out Jay whispered,

"G you have to now keep it strictly business with Sandra she is off limits, you have enough on your confused plate breaking that rule with Mia. Speaking of Mia, she called while you were in the studio and Mel is patiently waiting downstairs in the car for you."

In an attempt to bring his attention back to Mel.

Mel never questioning anything while he handled his business affairs allowed him to respond to a text, from Mia letting her know he had been in the studio and to make sure all was well. Mia's response came back fast, "All is well. Will I see you tonight?" Honesty being on the table at all times he responded that he would have company but tomorrow he would be available to do lunch. Normally she would respond right back but of course knowing he was going to be with someone else would delay that response. Waiting but no real urgency for her response it was like the pause button was released and Mel was all over him and this time she was the server. Gerald laid back in the seat as she unzipped his pants while looking up at him until she put all of him in her mouth making love to him with nothing but her mouth. This time he was the one fighting back the moan as she repeatedly took him all the way inside of her mouth with no stopping with a mission to complete her task. Her hands ran up under his shirt to rub his chest over his erect nipples which intensified his pleasuring. Not long before the return to his penthouse he released a moan and gave her what she was working for and she took every drop of it until his body stopped jerking. Her mission was complete and the anticipation of what the rest of the night was to bring, filled her mind putting a big smile on her face. She reached over in her purse and grabbed a wipe to clean him up still looking at him with nothing but a smile on her face as she watched him zip his pants back up. The limo pulled up and his phone finally chimed with a response from Mia,

"I have to check my schedule as far as lunch tomorrow. Have a good evening Mr. Livingston."

He was startled for a moment but so into Mel he just responded, "Ok". Jay called up to Maria to let her know they were downstairs as he grabbed Gerald's briefcase and umbrella to get Mel in from the rain as Gerald followed looking at her ass in that sundress. The doorman grabbed her shopping bags as they made their way to the elevator at exactly seven fifty-five, Gerald was a stickler for time and eight o'clock was his scheduled dinner time for the evening. Mia sent another text not so pleasant,

"Mr. Livingston you really need to do some soul searching and stop searching through my soul!"

Almost about to respond with the same tone but catching himself he responded,

"You are in a situation that clearly you are still not ready to fully let go of and you have made that painfully obvious at times through your words and actions clearly furthermore we both had an understanding that because of your situation and my situation that neither of us are looking for anything serious. So, your response has me a little confused. Actually, your responses and attitude have me questioning that now. What is it you actually want from me, from this?"

CHAPTER 9

"When the Heart Is Confused"

MARIA GREETED THEM AT THE door and the smell of dinner followed her as she took his briefcase, umbrella and let the doorman put Mel's bags down at the door as she asked Gerald,

"Mr. Gerald will you be eating at the table or in your room?"

Mel greeted Maria and headed back to the bedroom and Gerald followed her telling Maria the bedroom it is I guess, as Jay yelled see you in the morning. Almost forgetting Maria hadn't even brought the food in Mel slipped her shoes off and almost out of her sundress as Maria announced she was coming in carrying the food tray with their plates, a bottle of wine and two wine glasses. After she set everything up in front of the fireplace while Gerald turned on some music, she asked him would that be all for the evening. Gerald glanced over at Mel standing by the window looking out over the downtown traffic and told Maria he would be in good hands. Maria told them both good night as she exited the room and turned everything down but the dimmed overhead lights in the kitchen for the night knowing they wouldn't be leaving the room until her return in the morning.

Thinking they would be starving for dinner they picked right up from the limo. Mel's dress came off and Gerald peeled her open like a fresh orange. Gerald led her to the shower where he bathed her, and she bathed him and after that they stood in the middle of the shower and just held each other and kissed passionately. Not much was said the body language said it all as she massaged his shoulders and rubbed his back down to his now hard piece of peace as she liked to call it. He slowly turned her around to turn the tables from the car ride and returned the favor as he started rubbing her hard nipples and pressing against her so she could feel him against her tight perfect plump ass while lifting it just enough so he could enter into her tight wet walls. She leaned forward with her hands spread wide open as she leaned against the wall as he went deeper and deeper inside of her. This time there was nothing or no one stopping her from letting out her sexy moans of passion and cries of passion,

"Oh Gerald, oh Gerald deeper…"

with every word he answered deeper and deeper inside of her with every stroke. She did all she could to hold her climax, but the fight ended with her laying back into his arms and her head rested on his shoulder as he kissed her on her neck. He turned her around and stood there under the water kissing and holding each other until they showered again, and she told him round two wouldn't be such an easy conquer for him.

After they dried each other off they wrapped up in towels and they made their way to the now cold prepared plates with growling stomachs. Mel warmed up the food and fed Gerald like he was a king. The attraction from earlier in the day continued through-out the night and it was so different from the past months they had spent together. Mel had his every ounce of attention and Gerald was thinking things faster than he could say which puzzled him because he was always good with composing words while they both sat there on the oversized sofa listening to an all-female playlist ranging from Nancy Wilson to Lalah Hathaway to Ledisi to Jill Scott to Chante Moore to name a few. The intensity increased with every second that ticked around the clock. Mel removed the towel from his lap as she slid out of hers as well, leaned down and kissed him as if it were their wedding night. Gerald with no hesitance complied as her hands searched over his body like it was the first time, she ever touched him. Her hands moved between each defined line of his six pack as she kissed and pulled away to look him in his brown eyes and he in her seasonal green eyes as he went to say something, she stopped him and kissed him again in between pecks she said,

"You have me so close to Heaven right now and I never want it to end Gerald."

He rolled her over and laid her soft perfectly shaped body down letting his hands speak for him as he rubbed her body and caressed her mind with his every move. The arch of her back made her nipples line right up to his mouth as he sucked one and lightly pulled the other. Every pull of her nipple made her body jerk and she moaned out of passion as Minnie Riperton sang come, "inside of my love" he slid inside of her once again warm wet walls while looking in her eyes when they finally opened. In harmonic rhythm with Minnie, he took Mel to heights of intense love making. Before she climaxed, he lifted her up like a set of weights resting her legs wide open around his waist and her arms around his shoulders as he went deeper and she grinded on him until she hit her spot till she climaxed loud enough that if he had neighbors, they would have heard her and knew his name. Now limp her arms collapsed around his shoulders and her walls pulsated like a volcanic eruption happened inside of her. He carried her over to the bed and laid her pleased limped body down softly collapsing beside her.

"Hold me baby, please just hold me."

she softly whispered. Even if he was going to say no, he was to tired say it as he wrapped her up in his arms and they fell asleep.

Gerald's eyes opened around three a.m. as he looked down at Mel sleeping so peacefully on his chest and she nestled a little closer as if she felt him awaken and didn't want him to move. He looked up at the ceiling and his mind began to travel back to Nina and her text replaying it over and over again. Mia's text and the time they have spent together the closeness he felt to her, yet she said one thing and her last text said something else earlier. Mel had sparked something all day right into the evening they had just shared. Before tonight Mia was the close frontrunner if he had to make an immediate decision but he questioned was it more business and physical because today Mel sparked his heart, mind and soul it was a pure emotional exchange. He felt something he hadn't felt in months, someone had pierced his heart... and it was Mel. Glancing over at the nightstand he realized there was no condom used to possibly complicate things even more. For some reason he didn't panic and actually pulled her a little closer. Did Mel break that ice that was covering his heart since Nina had left him? He could actually feel it beating for the first time for someone who could help to mend it. What will he say when Nina reaches out again? What will Mia's mood be when they see each other? If he sees her? Sandra made her presence known at the studio with that last track. Still, he went back to Mel, her approach was so innocent, smooth, she had no baggage and seemed to have found the key to his heart and she did nothing special. The thoughts raced through his mind as he dozed off while still holding Mel.

CHAPTER 10

"The Pressure Is On"

THERE WAS NO MORNING TEXT from Mel because she was sound asleep next to him. Unusual for them to sleep in late but after the day before and the evening they had and no sound of the morning news on the tv Maria knew not to bother Gerald this morning. Jay stopped in to make sure he was alright since it was unusual not to see or hear anyone leaving the penthouse in the early a.m. to go to work not even a call for transportation. Maria was in the kitchen making a fresh pot of coffee waiting for the love birds to wake up before preparing Gerald's favorite Saturday morning breakfast which was scrambled cheese eggs, grits, turkey sausages and some home fries with fresh onions chopped up in them. Jay sat at the breakfast bar reading the newspaper and enjoying the site of Maria's ass moving around in the kitchen,

"Cup of coffee, Mr. Jay?"

He nodded yes as he held up his cup for a refill in his cup from home. She started her daily cleaning and dusting. The bedroom door opened and out came Gerald slowly walking down the hall with his head in his phone reading a long email from Mia. Jay knew by the slow walk and his head down in the phone that it wasn't business, and it wasn't good either. Hesitant to ask who or what it was he just chose to greet him with a simple good morning. Gerald just looked up in confusion and returned with,

"If you say so. Mia has lost her cool and I am not sure how to handle this one but to let her cool off for a minute. Strictly business from this point on before it gets ugly, if that is even possible."

Lost for words but relieved at the same time because it may be the break-away from one of the women and he could really focus on the one who could only really be good for Gerald. Keeping his composure Jay responded,

71

"Yes sir, will there be any special instructions on how to handle her?"

He went right into protection mode which is what made him the best at what he had been since the day he started securing Gerald. Before Gerald could give an answer, Mel was coming down the hallway in Gerald's robe bright eyed and bushy tailed, she snuggled right up under Gerald saying good morning to everyone and kissing Gerald on the cheek. Maria rushed over to start preparing their breakfast as Gerald slid a stool out for Mel then taking a seat himself.

"Your regular breakfast this morning Mr. G and Ms. Mel? Have some orange juice or a cup of coffee while I prepare it for you."

Both Gerald and Mel didn't hesitate to say yes to Maria as they both snickered like two kids. Jay looked up again and paid closer attention to how Gerald was rubbing Mel's hand while he looked at his phone and Mel talked to Maria while she cooked their breakfast. Gerald and Jay attempted to discuss some of his scheduling for the week ahead but it was obvious Gerald's attention was more focused on Mel than his schedule, so Jay changed the conversation to what the two of them were doing for the day. Maria announced breakfast was ready as she prepared their plates. Maria served them their plates and Jay made jokes of how Gerald made sure everything was alright and to Mel's liking before he began to eat. Maria refreshed their cups of coffee and went on dusting in the lounge area connected to the kitchen as she also took notice to the extra attention Gerald was paying to Mel this morning.

The two acted like Jay and Maria weren't even there so Jay took the hint and confirmed there was nothing scheduled for today and wanted to know if today would be an at home day. Gerald looked at Mel and told him they wouldn't be going out until dinner time so have Mr. Sam there by six o'clock and make reservations wherever Mel would like to eat tonight. Mel was just as stunned as she asked,

"Would you like to go to your cigar spot and just hang out tonight? Then we can come back to some of Maria's good cooking. I am fine with that baby. I am going to get my hair done on Monday so the smoke smell will be fine."

Mia chuckled and Gerald chuckled as well, so he had Jay to make the arrangements with Mr. Sam and Highland Cigars. Meanwhile Mel was rubbing Gerald feet with her feet under the breakfast bar like Maria couldn't see her doing it. Breakfast was finished rather fast, and the two lovebirds excused themselves, Jay took the hint they were definitely in lovebird mood,

"Jay we will see you at five forty-five."

Jay watched the two walk down the hall to the bedroom as Gerald walked behind her holding onto her by her hips and kissing her on her neck making Mel giggle. The faint voices of Gerald and Mel replied,

"See you at five forty-five Jayyyyyy."

acting like two kids in love. The door closed behind them and Jay and Maria looked at each other and laughed. Like the faithful and top-notch security, he pulled out his phone to make the arrangements and told Maria he would be back at five-thirty. Maria gave a thumbs up and a verbal acknowledgement as she watched his large from walk out the door.

No need for music from the speakers because the music was made from the soft passionate moans of the two lovers lost in each other again. Gerald handled her body cautiously as her mind went to a complete place of unexplainable pleasure. Like a maestro he wrote and composed music with her body and her moans encouraged him to continue. From a slow build up to a peak, down to a low and slow ending he handled her body gently as he let her down to rest like a kid who played on the playground all day, she fell asleep on his chest as she wrapped herself over him to be assured, he wasn't going anywhere. As usual he laid there thinking while he listened to the sound of her breathing while she peacefully slept. He felt guilty because for a minute he could see Mel in his life as his lady and the others would be a thing of his past but, would that make his decision just like Nina's decision to just leave him. Then he thought why he should even be thinking about Nina anymore she made her decision to leave him and get married and he had to let her, and their relationship go. Was this a sign that the heaviness he felt with the feelings about Nina was coming to an end and realizing Nina would always have a place in his heart, but could he ever get to the point that Nina was someone he loved deeply at one time in his life. It is time to move on, but he knew or was coming to grips with the fact that he would have to confront Nina in order to close that chapter of his life for good especially if he was even going to consider Mel would be his future. What would he do, what would he say when the time came to have a conversation with her? Could he do it face to face, would he even give her the satisfaction of talking to her face to face? At that moment Mia's words surfaced and yes, he realized in order to do anything or move on with anybody he would have to face Nina to finally be able to move on. He felt the fork in the road coming as he felt Mel's heartbeat on the side of his chest as he kissed her on the forehead. What was he going to do? When was he going to do it?

CHAPTER 11

"Can We Meet and Talk?"

AFTER A LATE NIGHT OUT at the cigar lounge which was filled with conversation and affection from the lounge to the car back to his place. The love making last night was even more intense than the night before probably the most intense since they had been together. The feelings were on high and it was a mutual exchange and the fact that no condom was used again just made things that much more intense. Climax after climax they battled like two tennis players in an intense tennis match for a championship title only, they knew about. This time Mel was the sure winner because it left Gerald motionless and in a deep sleep, Mel felt like she had been handed the gold cup title as she laid on him with a smile on her face. Maria knocked on the door wondering if they would be at least eating lunch since they had clearly slept through breakfast this morning. Mel responded because Gerald didn't hear her,

"Yes, we will need something to eat when he wakes up Maria"

with a slight giggle Maria assured Mel she would have something prepared. Jay was sitting at the breakfast bar reading the newspaper shaking his head as Maria entered the kitchen area. They both knew their employer must have had yet another heck of a late night and early morning.

Shortly after Maria finished doing her daily dusting and cleaning Gerald buzzed the intercom requesting a fresh salad and some water. Jay stepped over to the speaker to greet his boss and inquiring would he be leaving out today before Maria could confirm. A long pause and a faint answer came back,

"No but, Mel will be needing a ride to work at five thirty. I will need to sit down with you to discuss the schedule to come."

Looking at his phone that clearly already had the schedule posted he knew that was a code that either company was coming later, or he didn't want Mel to change her mind about going to work.

"Yes, sir I will see you at five fifteen to take Mel downstairs and afterwards we can sit down and discuss the schedule."

Maria prepared the salads and a sandwich for Jay as always. Knowing Jay was looking at her plump ass in her yoga pants as she moved around in the kitchen as he always did, she slowly turned around with a grin on her face as she put his plate on the counter. Unlike his boss Jay didn't have such a smooth approach when it came to women. The two of them carried on some small chat as he nervously finished his sandwich before he took one last peek at Maria before he left out until his return time of five-fifteen.

Maria was shaking her head at Jay being so shy but obvious with his peeking at her as she made her way down the hall with Gerald and Mel salads and water as requested. Maria's timing was perfect because Mel had just finished riding Gerald one last time before she had to start getting ready for work and pretty sure she had drained him this time as she looked back at him as she walked away slowly so he could see her phat ass and thick thighs on her way to take a shower. Maria knocked on the door before entering to bring them their late lunch. Gerald covered himself and told her to bring it over to the bed especially since he couldn't move.

"Maria you are worth every penny you requested and more. Thank you for your service, loyalty and respect. I will be staying in tonight if you would be so kind to prepare me something including some seafood?"

Maria responded,

"Thank you, Mr. G, for the opportunity and yes I will have dinner ready for you by six your regular dinner time, Si"

Maria responded in a nervous tone unsure where that conversation came from as she exited the room wiping her brow after she closed the door. Although she liked Gerald as her employer she was intimidated with his stardom and sometimes short straight demands.

The flashing light on his phone signaled a message was waiting. Who could it be with a frown on his face as he checked the text? It was two text messages, the first one was from Mia of course being strictly business and cold confirming a meeting on Monday and telling him to check his email for a file with some financials that required his signature. Not worried or affected at the moment he closed it and opened the next text message which was...Nina. The shower was still going so he opened it and in bold all uppercase letters it read,

"WE NEED TO TALK FACE TO FACE GERALD.
I NEED TO SEE YOU AND I WILL BE COMING
TO ATLANTA. YES, I KNOW WHERE YOU ARE,
CHRIS TOLD ME AND I HAVE SEEN YOU IN A FEW
TABLOIDS. PLEASE MEET WITH ME?"

That text stunned him like someone had taken his wind he fell back on the bed looking up at the ceiling as the sun shined through the skylights. Three attempts he made to respond finally on the fourth he was able to respond,

"I don't know why I should even be thinking about meeting you. You made your decision to leave me and everything that ever-symbolized US. I need to think about it, Nina and get back to you."

As soon as he pressed send the bathroom door opened to a naked Mel with a smile on her face,

"Well hello Mr. Livingston."

Unbelievably Gerald not only responded verbally but with a rise under the sheets satisfying Mel. Although very pleasing to her she had to decline it was nearing the time to start getting ready for work. Even after giving a quick glance again making her bite her bottom lip definitely wanting it again, she held firm and still declined and promised to take care of him and his friend at another time. Mel pointed at his salad and gestured him to eat as she made her way over to her overnight bag to begin to get dressed. Gerald gave it one more shot at trying to entice her for one-more round as he removed the covers to sit up to eat his salad, all she could do was smile and tell him no again. Gerald looked like a kid being told maybe next time at the toy store, so he sat all the way up to eat his salad giving her a pouting face. He held the fork in his hand, but it never touched the salad because he was completely distracted by her putting her lotion on her already soft skin watching her every movement until she slipped into her work uniform. Gerald was looking so pitiful that she came over and fixed his salad up for him and started feeding it to him. The staring started again, looking at her smooth skin a face with not one mark or blemish on it not looking a day over twenty-one, her now wet curly hair, tiny hands and her soft lips.

"Stop Gerald you know I have to go to work in an hour. Tell me when you want me back and I will be yours?"

77

The staring intensified again, Gerald took the fork from her pulled her in and kissed her on her neck to her lips. From the moan it was apparent her mouth declined but her body was saying something else as she fell in his arms.

"Gerald stop, I have to go to work you're not playing fair and you need to eat baby."

Playing safe this time she got up to finish getting dressed and getting her things together placing her overnight bag in the hallway after she opened the door for Maria to grab her things to put them at the front door. Checking her phone as she walked over with her arms open for a hug and Gerald pulled her between his legs and held her until she almost collapsed knowing full well, she would've agreed if he just said don't go.

Saved by the call from Jay that the car would be arriving in fifteen minutes as scheduled so Mel kissed him on his forehead and attempted to make her way to the safety of the front door pulling Gerald with her now that he was dressed in his robe. Offering a little resistance but he knew that once she left, he had to deal with Nina's message. Stopping her midway as they walked down the hallway, he pulled her close for a long kiss embracing her until her knees began to buckle. She had to pull away to catch her breath while gripping tightly onto Gerald's hand she bit her bottom lip gently while looking him directly into his eyes. Gerald whispered,

"Are you coming back tonight?"

Almost breathless as well as speechless, so she just nodded yes. Gerald made one last attempt to get Mel to stay and almost being caught midstream while trying to slip his hand into her work slacks Jay was standing at end of the hallway, cleared his throat and quickly chimed in that the car is here G. Like two kids had just finished sneaking a kiss they finished coming down the hallway to Jay standing there with a smile on his face and Maria in the kitchen. Maria told Jay where Mel's overnight and shopping bags were but before he could grab them Gerald instructed him, she would be returning tonight looking Mel in her eyes and never looked in Jay's direction. Mel was blushing so hard her face was beet red and she grabbed Jay by the hand as she led him to the door. Jay liked Mel the most out of all three of Gerald's web of women and it was evident at that moment as he grabbed her hand back and told her I got you, come on and they all laughed. It was quiet after they entered the elevator until Jay broke the silence,

"I will have Mr. Sam come back to pick you up at the end of your shift and I will meet you downstairs when you arrive."

Mel was spoiled by the attention from Gerald and now Jay as she blushed and thanked him. Once they were off the elevator and he saw that she was safely in the car on her way to work, Jay then headed back up to talk to Gerald.

Fresh out of the shower Gerald sat on the side of the jacuzzi looking out the window at the sunset wondering what he would say to Nina, what would she say to him, what did she have to say that could fix or explain her just leaving like she did. So deep in thought he didn't hear Jay knocking on the door,

"I'll be right out Jay."

While opening the text to read it again and reading it two more times before he responded. After typing three different responses he finally came up with,

"Nina, I am not sure what you could possibly have to say to me and why I am even entertaining the notion to meet up with you. Knowing it is a possibility that the huge hole you left in my heart will be re-opened where it has begun to close. Against my better judgement I will meet you to hear what you have to say. Let me know when is good for you and I will check my schedule."

Not expecting an immediate response his phone chimed there was a new message with Nina's response,

"I will be in Atlanta this week for a few days for business from Tuesday to Thursday and will be available any of those days after four."

Immediately afterwards another text came,

"Please don't stand me up Gerald or brush me off. I really would like the opportunity to talk to you more importantly I need to talk to you"

reading both he decided not to respond right away this time.

Jay knowing his boss very well he saw the distress on his face as he walked out of the bathroom knowing it had something to do with Nina or Mia and told him he had to do what was best for him at this time. Gerald just shook his head and told Jay he didn't feel like talking and he would be resting until Mel returned later. Jay didn't put up a fuss and just said he would check on him later as he walked out of the room as soon as he saw the hall light disappear Gerald sent a response,

"Wednesday at six send me a location and I will send a car for you wherever you are staying."

A quick response came back,

"Thank you, ok."

He laid back in the middle of his oversized king bed as the music played a soft playlist of sultry Phyllis Hyman ballads until he dozed off.

CHAPTER 12

"Why Should I Forgive You?"

GERALD WAS SOUND ASLEEP WHEN Mel entered from work and she didn't want to wake him. Slipped out of her uniform and walked in the bathroom right into the shower where she just sat under the water to do some thinking herself. Just like Gerald she was lost in so many mixed feelings from the past few days, Mel was beginning to develop feelings beyond what they had discussed and established. She was living in a moment that many women dream of and would give to be in, but it was also one that had no guarantee of a happy ever after. She was deeper in than she even wanted to admit to herself. The very vision of him and the sound of his voice melted her. His large soft hands caressed her body and his soft lips left imprints below the surface of her skin wherever he placed them, when he entered her body every alarm sounded in her body, he was the closest thing to Heaven she was sure and had ever felt from any man she had been with. Just sitting there her body warmed and she could feel the moistness of her pussy begin to run down her inner thigh just thinking about him.

She sat there longer than she realized as the water told her so because it began to cool so she showered and got out to a steamy room only to be greeted by her dream, only if the dream was to completely come true. Gerald took her towel off and pulled her into his arms and held her not saying a word as she let out a soft sigh of relief and laid her head on his chest. For what seemed to be eternity they just stood there holding each other looking like a finely sculpted piece of black love art. It was evident everything she was just thinking about he felt the same way. Was she going to say something or just stand there in his arms continuing to take in the moment, she decided to just lay on his chest and squeezed tighter and the gesture was met as he squeezed her back. Like a little doll baby Gerald picked her up in his arms and carried her to the bed with her head laid on his shoulder which were like firm pillows. Laying her down slowly on the bed he lifted and opened her legs sliding into her until her back arched as it always did because of the size of his piece of peace as she called it. Like a master painter he painted another new masterpiece inside of her walls with his paint brush with his every stroke her canvas received his every stroke. She wrapped her legs around his waist and pulled him in deeper and closer to hold him while kissing his neck as he moaned in her ear and she exhaled

"Gerald, Gerald, Gerald ummm baby"

and her body tensed up as she was about to climax. His strokes intensified as his breathing did and he moaned her name, Mel. Every muscle in his body tightened as they climaxed together like something had taken all of the air out of him, he covered her little body as her legs fell open to the sides of him.

Silence filled the air as they silently laid there in the bed with Mel now on his chest. Hesitant to say anything Mel asked,

"Gerald what are we doing? What is happening between us? We have moved in a direction beyond what we said in the beginning. You have made love to me for two days with no condom and the past four months you have been simply amazing to me in every fashion imaginable. What is going on?" Almost like she read his mind he was lost for words he was finally able to respond,

"Mel, I don't know, I really don't know. I don't have an answer but, I do know that you have reached and began to mend my broken heart and that is a place I was guarding since my breakup. If it is something that you aren't able to handle in regard to me being unsure of right now or not ready for anything, please let me know. I am confused right now but I know that I don't want you to leave, and I don't want to lose you. I know that is unfair to you and I never want to hurt you or put you in an uncompromising position with your feelings."

All she could say was,

"Gerald, baby I am not going anywhere until you tell me otherwise. Am I afraid, yes. I would be lying to you if I said anything else. But I can tell you at this moment I am not going anywhere."

Not another word was spoken they just laid there holding each other until they dozed off. What has he gotten himself into and has he gotten in over his head with Mel at this moment in their time together? Still no word from Mia since her angry text messages which could be the sign that she was getting tired of their situation outside of the business portion. It wouldn't be that simple to just exit from her at the moment because there was unfinished business and of course she would require much less deserved a conversation if that was his decision for sure. In all fairness with her knowing how Nina's break up left him with so many mixed emotions Mia always said she wouldn't want to do the same to him but, there was always that question in her mind would she allow him to do the same to her. The open relationships that he was involved in since he had come to Atlanta Gerald was able to maintain his stand that he was single and not going to answer to anyone nor was he looking for anything serious. Like any situation or relationship that included the act of sex feelings are bound to change especially when there is little to no presence of condoms being used. The use of a condom was important to lower the risk of sexually transmitted diseases as well as pregnancy but something deeper than that was complications of unprotected sex could intensify feelings and emotions from both parties involved was something his Mom preached about from his younger to his adult years. He was sure that his Mom was looking down on him with great disappointment with his lack of responsibility in regard to the use of condoms not with just one but with all three of these women at times.

For the next two days Gerald cancelled all of his plans and meetings and stayed in his room and bed with Mel only getting up to shower and eat. Gerald answered all of his emails and calls from the bed or the sofa. Mel was very attentive and receptive to his every need sometimes not even allowing Maria to bring the food to the room she served him herself. They talked about his past as far as his relationship with his Mom and the non-existent relationship with his Father as well as his breakup with Nina. Some topics up until now only Nina knew about that made Mel feel like there could be actually be a future but she cautiously remained in her lane and followed his lead. It was Tuesday night the night before he was to meet Nina to talk. Which was the one thing he didn't tell Mel about in the midst of all they talked about over the past two days. It was the best two romantic days they had spent together without sex being a main focal point of their time in each other's company. It was a breakthrough for them both that was evident, and they were for sure taking a turn down a road that surely different from what they had both agreed upon. After their conversation they sat in front of the fireplace and had dinner by candlelight while some soft jazz music playing. Gerald kept Mel smiling and she returned the feeling as well. After dinner they cuddled up under a blanket on the sofa and fell asleep until the morning.

The sun rose and finally Wednesday morning arrived and as if Mel knew he was going to meet Nina she put it on him in the bed, the shower and the bed again before they were able to get out to start their first day apart in two days. Jay knew Gerald had dug in deeper with Mel, but it didn't look like he was worried at all the way the two of them were all over each other and finishing each other sentences while they ate breakfast. They left out right after eating and Gerald let Maria know he would be home for dinner so she could prepare something for dinner as they exited the penthouse. They held hands on the elevator and continued to hold hands as they walked out of the elevator and the pictures started snapping and unlike all the other times, he didn't try to make the picture taking hard to take of him with this mystery lady on his arm and he wore a big smile on his face, inside Jay was smiling just as much as Gerald. Jay held his normal position securing them from behind as Mr. Sam pulled close to the curb. Holding the door open Jay let Gerald know they had to make a stop at Mia's office. Puzzled but still the look of no worries on Gerald's face, he just gave a head nod of ok and got in the car as the pictures continued to snap. The car pulled off while Mel checked her make-up and uniform in preparation for work as Gerald sat across from her looking at her from head to toe his eyes were glued to her uniform perfectly fit her figure as her hips and thighs exposed themselves through her work slacks. She looked up and caught him staring,

"Can I help you with something sir? Do you see something you like Mr. Livingston?"

with her smile that melted Gerald every time and with a boyish grin he just shook his head and replied,

"Yes, to both questions Ms. Mel, you can help me with all of it and yes I damn sure see something that I like and want."

Leaning in for a kiss he pulled her over to his side of the limo and hugged her, she exhaled,

"Stop, I have to go to work today and you have business to tend to as well."

Saved by the partition window coming down and the sound of Jay's voice telling them they were five minutes away from her job. Mel fixed her blouse and reapplied her lipstick again so she could be ready to exit the car as she waited for him to tell her next time she would be seeing him. The car stopped and shortly after Jay was there to open the door just as she leaned over for one more kiss,

"I'll send for you tonight at the end of your shift, ok."

Full eye contact until she exited as he grabbed her ass. Blushing she told Jay,

"See you later Jaaaaaaayyyyy"

Jay replied,

"Ummm hummm see you later Miss Melllll. Have a good shift."

The door closed and Gerald sat back in the seat as his phone vibrated and it was Nina,

"You can pick me up from the Convention Center we are finishing early today so I can be out front around two thirty. I am looking forward to seeing you."

The text read. Unlike the past few text exchanges his response was calm,

"I will be there at three o'clock."

The sounds of Raheem DeVaughn played as the car merged back into the Peachtree St. traffic now headed to Mia's office. What would the mood be like with Mia and was it one he should even be worried about right now? Gerald pulled his phone back out and scrolled through the news websites until they arrived at Mia's office. Mia was standing in the window of her third-floor office. A look of disgust and hidden happiness was the combination that was expressed on her face. Jay followed Gerald in pass the front desk avoiding contact with the people in the lobby straight to the elevator with Jay right behind him as always. The elevator stopped at the third floor where they were greeted by Mia in a fitted black thigh length skirt. Even in black you could see her figure and her walk was just as enticing,

"Well, well, well Mr. Livingston, how are you? Jay he is in safe hands I am here alone today. Relax and watch some tv."

in her smart firm but professional tone. Gerald followed Mia into her office and took a seat in front of her desk like a kid in the principal's office who knew he was about to be scolded for his actions for not coming to class for over three almost four days. Instead, Mia shot straight for the throat and kept it business discussing the completed acquisitions as well as the ones still in the working. She stayed behind her desk because if he touched her it would break her business mode and she knew she would melt right there in his arms. A combination of disgust and desire was exchanged as they discussed business and future ideas. Gerald looked down at his Vintage Movado watch to check the time remembering he had a meeting with Nina. Being the keen sharp witted one Mia said,

"Well, we are pretty much done here, and I am sure you have another stop or two to make before you go home."

He chuckled listening to her fish around to see if she would get an invite for later on but before he could even respond she stopped him,

"I've seen the tabloids and the entertainment news she must be special if you are taking pictures and not hiding your face. Before you go just remember what I said to you, address your previous and current hurt before you hurt someone else because I don't think you're ready for a relationship. At least until you address your past. Be fair to her and yourself, please."

The phone rang and she answered it just like what he may have had to say would mean nothing, putting the call on hold she let him know she would wait for his call on the decisions that needed to be made and would have the numbers and information he requested forwarded to him. Like a shock he was startled because she pulled one of his endings on him, back to business. As he walked out of the office Mia looked at his broad back in his tailored suit biting her bottom lip hoping he wouldn't turn around. As he held the door open looking back at her, she put her head down to the desk and opened the files and continued with her call so he wouldn't know she was checking him out. He said goodbye and he would talk to her later.

Jay looked down at his watch in total disbelief that he didn't have to peel him away from Mia to make it on time to pick up Nina. Gerald asked Jay to find him a good sandwich shop because he had an hour to burn. While they were on the elevator of course someone recognized him, which lead to a few autographs until they got off the elevator and made it to the car. Checking his text of course one from Mel which made him smile ear to ear, Sandra was the next on the log concerning business both professional and personal. Sandra's text received a quick response of acknowledgment of receipt and will get back to her at his earliest convenience. He scrolled back to Mel's text and smiled Jay could read the look on his face and said,

"She got them hooks in you and you don't even know it yet G."

They both chuckled as Gerald typed his response while smiling the whole time. As soon as he hit send it was instantaneous that they responded back and forth and this went on for about ten minutes. Nina's text came and the smile quickly turned to a frown. Nina let him know she would be ready in an hour at the Convention Center at the three o'clock time he gave her. Jay had Mr. Sam stop for his sandwich as he requested and then headed to Nina. The ride was silent while he ate his sandwich. The downtown traffic was smooth sailing every light was green. To ease the tension Jay confirmed Ms. Mel needing a pickup this evening. Gerald let him know she was getting off early so they would be heading to her as soon as he finished with Nina. Five minutes away from our location Mr. Sam announced, Jay saw the change in his posture, and he could tell Gerald was nervous, so he asked,

"Are you ok, and will you be ok? This is the first time you have seen her since she left you." Gerald mumbled,

"As alright as I am going to get and very unsure of what this is going to do in regard to my still open feelings for her. Jay, I don't know, I just don't know."

With that being said Jay left it alone and as the car stopped Jay got out to stand position for Nina to come out of the building. Not recognizing her because she had cut hair short, and she was wearing makeup something she never did because she didn't have to.

"Hello Jay has it been that long that you forgot what I looked like?"

Remaining in his neutral zone as always, he smiled and made mention to the change in her hairstyle while complimenting it as well as he opened the door for her to get in and requesting her bag as she did so. Like two deer caught in headlights they stared at each other for what seemed about five straight minutes trying to see who would say something first. Nina broke the silence,

"Gerald, hello. How are you doing?"

another pause as Nina stared at the man she was once in love with for almost eleven years as Gerald looked out the window.

"Gerald it is so much I want to say, first I have to say I am sorry for how I handled things with you and the way I ended our relationship. You left me no other choice, for years I waited for a wedding...I had it all planned out, what I would say and how I would say it to you. Now that I am here all I can say is I am sorry, I am so sorry Gerald."

As the tears rolled down her face which at one time would melt him led to a cry as Gerald just leaned over to give her some tissue with no emotion at all and still had nothing to say,

"Gerald you don't have anything to say. I know I hurt you and you have to have something to say."

The car began to move, and Gerald was still speechless not even making eye contact. Turning to the side to hide the tears he finally asked her,

"What do you have to say? What are you expecting me to say? You fucking left me, left me with a fucking letter like I did something so wrong that you couldn't tell me face to face. I gave you the world and would have given you the planets and everything else in the solar system. You have married and moved on all in less than a year after you left me. You want to know what I have to say? Nothing. You need to be doing the talking, all the talking"

Nina wept but got it out,

"Will you actually listen or just pacify me for the time I am here with you? Gerald, we played house for over ten years with no children or a wedding date. You're right, I was wrong, and I am so wrong for how I left. As far as the moving on portion of my wrongdoing. I knew my now husband from work and yes, we were friends and yes, he was there when you were on the road or your long nights at the studio. There were no intentions to do anything past friends and co-workers. It was nothing until I left you before we began dating. It has been one of the worst mistakes I have ever made. He is nothing like he portrayed, now I am married to a man who is mentally, physically and verbally abusive, very possessive and not on my level at all. He is a well-dressed animal, and I am sitting here now with the man I should have never left. I guess I am getting my painful dose of karma. I am so sorry, and I pray that you will find it in your heart to forgive me. Gerald I still love you and I have made the worst decision of my life."

There was another long pause and the look on his face that Nina knew so well which helped her to prepare for what was to come out of his mouth from a painful and hurt place she put in his heart. Slow to anger but when it came, he could cut you with mere words and rarely used profanity which she was sure was already out the window for this situation.

"So, you feel this apology will clear the hurt and pain that you have caused my heart? It took me damn near, no over a year to even come out of my condo. You left me with a letter and a broken heart. You shattered my heart into a million tiny pieces. We wouldn't even be having this conversation if you were happy and he equaled up to what he promised you he would be. I poured every ounce of sweat into you and all I deserved was a letter to tell me you had left me then a smack in the face of you getting married not long after you left me. You knew my fears and holdbacks about marriage, but we were so close, and you did what my father did to my mother minus a mystery kid. You have come here and for what? To add insult to injury. I have finally been able to smile and accept that we...we, you and I will never be again. Now you have dropped this on me that you are with an animal who hurts you. For that part I am sincerely sorry Nina, I am hurt that you are being abused... (it was like a soft whisper about the conversation that he and Mia had the other night made him change his tone and posture from cold to concerned) I think that you need to get out of that situation and soon before he really hurts you...no one deserves that."

Gerald paused long enough to tell Jay to give them some more time to talk as the car came to a stop. The tears began to flow, and Gerald handed her more some tissue. They just sat there across from each other; Gerald felt so many emotions as he thought of the best way to say what he knew needed to be said to her. He sat back in his seat and took a deep breath before he spoke,

"Nina, I must admit I had so many more mean things that I wanted to say to you today, but I have to restart my conversation with I am sorry, I am sorry that I let my unresolved issues in my past cause you to feel as though the best thing for you to do was to leave me, just walk away. I also want to apologize for not fully taking your feelings and needs into consideration. I was so afraid of becoming the man that my father was that I lost the one person who meant the world to me. Sadly, it took for you to leave me and a conversation with a now friend of mine to take a look at the part I played in your decision to move on without me. There have been many days I felt like my world was over and I would never love again after us. You were my world and everything in it, but I learned that I fell short pass the physical gifts while trying to give you the world when all you really wanted was me and I am sorry. I pray that someday you will love again as well and given some time to heal I hope that we can at least be able to be friends at some point. I really want you to think seriously about getting out of that marriage you are in right now. You do not deserve that type of man and he damn sure don't deserve a woman like you. You damn sure don't deserve the treatment you are getting."

He took a deep breath of relief as his racing heart began to calm down. Nina's face was soaked from the tears that never stopped. She looked at him and said she wished that she had just had a conversation with him and maybe just left to let himself get himself together to see what he just shared with her. He patiently waited for her to get herself together so she could respond, as she did the tears still flowing,

"Gerald, I just wished that I could have the day back that I wrote that letter. I know I hurt you and I want you to know that I am hurting now seeing you here today because like you said there could never be another time for us...I will take the advice you have given me today and separate myself from this man. I feel like I have gotten what I needed today, and I can start the process to start my life over once again without you and him. Thank you for seeing me and more over that you have accepted your part in our breakup. I know this will take some time, but I hope that we can at least be friends. I know that there is still hurt when it comes to me and that I understand. I will always love you and I will always cherish the time that we were together."

She smiled a little behind the tears and leaned forward extending her hand for his and he leaned forward extending his hand to her then he pulled her to him and hugged her as he whispered, I am sorry, Nina. He felt his heart release the anger he had been harboring since she left even up to the moment she first got in the car and he offered her his place to stay if and when she did decide to leave her now husband. Gerald let her go so she could sit back and get herself together. Still parked in front of the Marriot Hotel he made light of the situation by offering to grab a cup of coffee in the restaurant in the hotel so they could talk some more. A turn of events that Jay didn't expect but was happy that it was happening because he knew that if Gerald didn't address the anger and hurt, he fought with off of his chest there was a great chance that it would just make way for someone else to be hurt by him again. It would also continue to fester and continue to grow in him, and he would just be more like the man he wanted so much not to be like to another woman knowing what his Mom went through when his Father left them with no notice. Jay walked them inside and saw to them getting a table and he sat the bar until Gerald was done.

Nina kept apologizing and just kept saying that she wished she had just talked to him instead of leaving the way that she did. Gerald thanked her for apologizing but he accepted his part as well and asked her to please stop apologizing because he was in the wrong as well. They spoke for another hour or so and his last request was that she seriously consider getting some help and once again extended his place to her again along with anything else that he could do to help her out of her situation if she decided to make a break from her husband. He helped her out of her seat and hugged her as he told her,

"I will always love you and I too am sorry for the way that our relationship ended. I wish you the best and if you need anything, Nina…anything let me know."

Nina hugged him and let out a sigh of relief and the tears had stopped. When they released each other, she looked up at him and told him,

"Thank you, Gerald, thank you so much. I will let you know when I make my move and if I will need to take you up on the offer in regard to staying in your place. You just told me what I already knew, I need to get out of my marriage, and I thank you for talking to me today."

They left out of the restaurant and walked to the elevator and hugged one last time until the elevator opened. Gerald told her to be careful and that he would have the condo cleaned out for her in case she needed to stay there for however long she needed. Nina turned around and smiled as the elevator doors closed. Jay called out to tell Mr. Sam they were on their way out and the next stop was to pick up Mel from work. Jay, I need to talk I need you sit in the back with me on the way to Mel. Once they were in the car Gerald didn't waste a second expressing his feelings. He told jay that he needed to really thank Mia for what had just happened because she was the one who stressed that he take a look at his part that he played in Nina making the decision to just up and leave. He said he had struggled with what he was going to say to Nina and he truly planned on giving her a piece of his mind placing all the blame on her, but he realized that it was his fault combined with the hurt he carried for his Father and how he broke his Mom's heart only to do the same with a woman he physically didn't leave but wasn't really there the way she wanted him to be and as a result he pushed her away. He told Jay he apologized and that if she needed anything to please him know. He even shared that he extended her a place to stay in his condo until she figured out what she wanted to do when and if she leaves her husband. Jay frowned until he told him that her husband was both mentally and physically abusing Nina. He felt it was the least he could do because if he had just done the right thing, they wouldn't be in the two places where they are now. Jay asked,

"But honestly G, how do you feel now that you have seen her and got everything off your chest? Are really ready to move on now or are you going to take some real time without the three women that you are currently dating and get yourself together now that you realize your part that you played in your break-up? I am both happy and a bit surprised with the outcome, but I feel like it was much needed so that you can move on with your own life. All I ask is don't let guilt further impair you from moving on as well."

Gerald responded,

"One step at a time Brotha now tell Mr. Sam to take me to get my Mel, please."

Jay agreed and Gerald laid back in the seat and closed his eyes as the tears rolled down his face.

CHAPTER 13

"Where Do We Go from Here?

JAY TOOK A LOOK AT his watch realizing it wasn't time to pick Mel up yet and asked how they were picking Mel up now because it wasn't time for her to be getting off work as Gerald turned his phone around showing Jay, he was texting her to see if she could leave early,

"Mel, I need you, please, please leave work early if you can?"

Jay knew it was serious and asked, was he ok and was that the last of Nina? Slow to respond but with firmness,

"As far as anything beyond being her friend if that was even possible, yes. Jay I will always love her, but she is now married, an unhappy and in an unhealthy marriage that she needs to get out of but that is her decision to make. I told her that if there was anything that I could do to help her I would and I shared with you that I even offered her my place if she needed somewhere to stay. Other than that, that is it for us."

Jay knew that Gerald had been hurting since Nina left but seeing her and talking to her no matter what else was said may have been the beginning to what he needed to fully move on and would hopefully make him be more cautious than what he had been up till now as far as the women he had connected himself to since he had come to Atlanta. Mr. Sam buzzed in to let him know they were fifteen minutes from Mel's job. The end of the rush hour traffic was still moving slow which was good so that he could get himself together before they arrived to pick Mel up if she was able to leave work early. Still no response from Mel he instructed Mr. Sam to just pull into the garage and wait when they arrived. Still thinking about all that had been said and questioning what he was going to do now and what he was going to say to Mel when she asked him what is wrong. Finally, a response from Mel letting him know she would be able to leave in about thirty minutes and to meet her in the garage. A quick response came right afterwards,

"Gerald what is wrong?"

Gerald just responded without immediately giving off a sign that something was surely wrong,

"Mel, I need you baby, please. See you in thirty minutes I will be in the garage by the elevators."

Gerald sent Chris a text while they waited for Mel to say hello and letting him know he may be back in Chicago in the next month or so for business and he would like to see him and his family. Chris still mad but was open to the idea responded he would like that and would be awaiting his word and wishing him well in Atlanta. Chris asked if Nina had reached out to him because he gave her his whereabouts and planned to be in Atlanta. Gerald just gave a short and direct answer that he heard from her, they met up to talk and everything went well, and they were able to close their chapter on good terms. Chris didn't pry any and responded short and direct that he was happy to hear and sure they would speak on the conversation when he was ready to talk about it.

The thirty-minutes passed and with both anticipation and excitement to see Mel as she made her way to the car greeted by Jay with the limo door open. As soon as she entered the car Gerald pulled her in and hugged her like none of the other hugs before. She held him and asked,

"Baby, what is wrong? Please talk to me?"

There was a long pause, and the hug was just as long and tight. After about ten minutes into the ride finally Gerald said,

"Baby what are we doing? I am in need of you and all the comfort that only you can give me. I need to talk but I don't want to talk right now, I just need you to be here. Am I asking too much? If I am, I am sorry."

Mel pulled away to look at his face and she could see he was troubled about something and she reassured,

"I am here baby, I told you that I am here until you tell me otherwise and mean every word of it."

as she then pulled him into her arms this time for the rest of the ride to his place. The only thing that could be heard was their breathing and the rush hour traffic. Gerald was thinking about her and she was thinking about him as they stared out of the window. Mel was beginning to fear if he was about to tell her he no longer wanted whatever they had between them. Gerald was about to call Maria to tell her to prepare some dinner, Mel stopped him reminding him she was preparing dinner because he asked her this morning. Right at that moment she really knew he was not himself and it was something serious. He closed his eyes, and she rubbed the side of his face until he dosed off until she woke him up,

"Baby, wake up we are here."

the door opened and Jay helped Mel out of the car while grabbing Gerald's briefcase and followed them close in tow as they entered the building holding hands Mel was getting use to the whispers about the star who lived in the penthouse on the top floor. The elevator ride was silent until they exited, and Gerald told Jay he would be in for the night and pretty much all day tomorrow. Swiping his key to let Mel in he turned around to tell Jay,

"I am good Jay I just need to make some serious decisions"

a brotherly hug and their childhood handshake and Jay closed the door after Gerald walked in. The smell of food cooking and the sound of Maria and Mel in the kitchen speaking in their native Spanish tongue filled the kitchen as he walked by to go to his bedroom. Candles were already lit, and the bed was pulled back, so he just plopped down and kicked off his shoes shortly after Mel walked in with his tray of food. Before he could say a word or lift a finger, she motioned him to relax by putting her hand on his shoulder and told him she was going to take good care of him. She stood him up and undressed him which was rare that he even sat on the bed with his clothes on because he was a stickler for anyone sitting on his bed with their clothes on that they had worn outside. She went and grabbed a wet washcloth to wipe his face and hands before she fed him some baked chicken, mashed potatoes, asparagus and homemade biscuits. With every fork full he looked her in her eyes with thoughts of what he would say.

After the meal Maria came in to get the tray and let him know she would be staying in her quarters tonight if he needed anything. Relieved but anxious at the same time he once again asked Mel,

"What are we doing? Where are we going with this? I feel things for you I thought I wouldn't ever feel again, not even sure I even wanted to allow myself to feel, and I don't want to mislead you or be mis lead."

Mel's heart raced and her words stumbled like a child learning to walk for the first time. Finally, she was able to say,

"Gerald I... I too have feelings that I didn't have any plans on having for and with you. I have fallen in love with you, who you are beyond Gerald Livingston the world knows and how you have treated me since our first night together and I must admit I am scared. I knew the rules and that there was to be no feelings attached but I am in love with you and I cannot hide it. So, my question as well is...where are we going?"

Gerald just grabbed her and pulled her in as close as he could get her without hurting her from squeezing her too tight,

"Mel, I have feelings that are identical to yours right now and have had them for quite some time and I don't want to lose you because of my foolishness with these other women that mean nothing to me at the end of their stay. Nothing compares to what I feel when you are with me and when I know you are about to leave me. It was because of my unaddressed fear of abandonment that cost me my previous relationship/engagement and I don't want that to happen ever again."

Mel responded,

"Is this about your ex-fiancé? What happened today after you left me?"

The tears flowed and he told her of the meeting and conversation he had with Nina before he came to her. The pain and the relief it brought, the closure it brought and the door it opened to finally be able to say he was ready to move on. Was he ready to move on to marriage, not at this time but never would he do it the way he did with Nina and lose another wonderful woman, but he knew she was the quality of woman he wanted to call his mate and bear his children if given the opportunity.

The candles burned out and the sun was rising as they laid in each-other arms from the hours of conversation until they fell asleep. Both awakened facing each other and neither knew what to say to each other so there was nothing but silence. Finally, Gerald kissed Mel on her forehead and asked her to take the day off he would pay her salary for the day if would mean a yes. Mel declined the money but agreed to take the day off if they would spend the day talking about the direction they were going in and how it would happen. Gerald was sure Mel would still have many questions, some he was ready to answer and some he would have to make himself ready to answer. Still hesitant to say anything that may cause a question to be asked Gerald continued to lay in silence but mentally prepared for what was to come. Mel did the same, unprepared for what she may hear but she began to ask her first question.

"Why do you want me or why would you want to be with me? When you could have any woman in the world."

She waited for his answer and Gerald responded,

"Melanie, you are everything opposite of what I expected to find in the midst of my foolishness messing with you and two other women at the same time. You haven't asked for anything and turned down everything I have offered to you but myself. Even on nights you knew I was in the company of someone else you didn't act the fool the next time we were in the company of each other, and you also still sent your daily morning text every single morning. It was and is the small things you have done that have landed us here today. I have to be honest I met my ex yesterday to close that chapter of my life so that I could start the next chapter fresh. I was able to acknowledge my fault in the demise of our relationship. I have learned from my mistake and I know that in order to get through my fear of being like my father and my fear of abandonment I have to face it and I cannot put you or anyone else in a position that would make you want to leave me. I want you to be in this next chapter and chapters to come and hopefully the rest of my life story..."

Mel interrupted,

"I am flattered but scared at the same time. You have some unfinished business with these other women and is the ending with your ex the reason you want to be with me? I am crazy about you and I have been one of the mystery women until the past few days when we exit the building or wherever we are spotted. This is all new to me, dating a celebrity and knowing I wasn't the only one. I never thought I would be in an open relationship so to speak. You have shown me so much love and affection in such a short time as well as taken my body to places I never thought existed. You have to understand and respect my questions and fears."

Gerald got up and walked over to the window looking out at the streetlights and the busy streets full of cars and people walking as he thought of his response, he took a deep breath before he responded,

"Baby you have every right to feel this way and I have to show you that I want to be with you and only you if you allow me into that space. Please don't let my actions these past months scare you away now that I am ready to make an exclusive relationship with you, I didn't plan on any of this happening with you or anyone else. I know that my career may be discouraging as well and can assure you that my situation with my ex is over for good both mentally and physically. She has moved on and married. Our conversation today was clear that there will never be another opportunity for a rekindle of us and to be honest I knew that just didn't want to really face it. To be totally honest with you she is in an abusive relationship and I offered my place in Chicago if she needed a place to stay if she decides to leave her husband. It was the least I could do but if that is a problem, I will tell her it's not a good idea. Just to clear up the other women it is just two of which one is married but separated and knows that someone fully has taken her place which is you. The other is an artist which once I sign will be strictly business only, a rule I live by. Relationships and business never work out and I do not cross that line at all. Most importantly your consistency and your heart are what has made me realize that it is you that I need in my life now and someday soon, forever."

Mel smiled but then inquired more about Mia and what would happen between them if they decided to become exclusive, Gerald was honest about her being his real estate agent and broker for all of his business ventures who was still married but separated.

The more they talked nothing was left a secret which was good but not so good watching Mel's tense stance changed a few times with tears rolling down her face as she sat in the middle of the bed with her legs crossed with a pillow between them looking Gerald straight in his eyes. Maria had been to the room twice to see if they needed anything and Gerald sent her away. Jay checked in as well but was also sent away as well. After the soft but firm grilling of Gerald, Mel opened up about who the woman he wanted to start a chapter with, and she made it clear that she felt the same way about being with him. They were a few years apart in age, she was a college graduate and the first one to graduate anything in her family. She shared that the few men she had been with either turned out to be married, in a relationship, used her for her body and the perks that came with her working for the hotel. She talked herself into more tears as she talked about her life and Gerald consoled her reassuring her that the heartbreaks would be no more if she gives him the opportunity, the hurt will be no more, unlike the others before him. He loved her for the woman she had shared with him up to this point and wanted to get to know more about her and wanted her in his life for her spirit and soul which was in addition to her heart. He shared with her that she had touched him in places he thought he blocked off for what he thought would be forever. By this time, they were both with tears running down their faces. She asked him one last time what,

"Baby, what are we doing here? I cannot take being hurt again Gerald. Please don't do that me. I can be your friend and nothing else, I promise you I won't be some crazed, hurt bitch who makes life difficult for you."

They fell asleep holding each other after four more hours of confessions and conversation. Mel awakened before Gerald and when he opened his eyes, she kissed him and told Gerald firmly,

"Baby before you can commit to me or anyone else you have to tie up your loose ends and yes, I want that anyone to be me. So, where we are going from this point all depends on what you do."

All he could say was okay as he kissed her on the forehead. Pulling her closer to him and they dozed back off to sleep.

CHAPTER 14

"How Do I Tell Him?"

GERALD AWAKENED BEFORE MEL AND after sliding out of the bed without waking her he went into the bathroom where he stirred in the mirror searching for the words he would say to Mia and Sandra telling them that his heart now had a new owner. He showered and stayed quiet while he slipped on something to lounge in while Mel was still asleep which was strange for her to sleep late. The smell of Maria's cooking made the next set of steps for Gerald to the kitchen. There was Maria doing what she did best, cooking breakfast and preparing dinner.

"Good morning Sir, will you be eating now or waiting for Ms. Mel?"

Gerald let her know he would be waiting for the lady to wake up as he picked up the morning paper. The sun shined in through the huge smoked glass windows so bright and warm. Today was different he wasn't thinking about Nina at all and looked at the cartoons instead of stocks or the entertainment sections first. Closure had been accomplished seeing and talking to Nina and he wasn't going bury to it unaddressed like he did everything else in his life that hurt him. Jay entered at his daily check in time of eight o'clock to see if there were any changes to the free day. Gerald confirmed today would be a relax day, but they would be going to Chicago for a few days there were a few things he needed to take care of, and Jay jokingly asked,

"We're not going back how you came here are we, on the bus?"

Gerald burst out in laughter and assured him the bus was not how they would be traveling back. Jay and Maria made their little innocent greeting as she slid him an egg, cheese and turkey bacon sandwich which was his favorite. Gerald chuckled because he knew that Jay liked her, and Jay tapped him on the leg to stop. Little did they know Maria was smiling over at the stove with her back towards them it seemed Jay wasn't the only one who had a liking going on. Gerald continued to read his paper hiding his chuckle.

Mel had awakened now just lying there every so often looking around the room and wondering if it would be her place, she would call home, or would it be another man she would see set her to the side for another woman. She curled up in a ball and began to shed a few tears because this time she not only really liked this man, but she was in love with this man and after the conversation they had last night she dreamed of a life with him, but she painfully was willing to walk away if he chose to keep things as they are. She knew what she was getting herself into in the beginning and she accepted the terms with no thoughts that any of what was happening would ever happen because she too had given up on love. Yes, she is a drop-dead gorgeous Georgia Peach but her chances of being the wife of a man of Gerald's caliber and many talents of being a singer, songwriter, producer, real estate mogul and now broker just wasn't in the cards for her or so she thought. World known for his lyrics Gerald could have any woman he wanted if for nothing else his physical appearance would allow him to be with any woman he desired. The questions began to fill her head again, what if he does all they discussed and if he meant that they were really going to be together? What if after he does clear the loose ends and says he's still not ready? Hearing his voice sometimes raised the hairs on her neck. His touch melted her down to her frame and his kisses made her wet in every aspect any woman would love. The doubt battled the security that he really wanted her just as much as she wanted him.

She wiped her tears as she heard Gerald's voice getting closer to the bedroom door and she tried to straighten herself up before he came into the room.

"Why didn't you let me know you were awake baby?" Breakfast is ready and I was waiting for...wait a minute why are you crying?"

Mel tried to deny she was crying as the tears swelled up in her eyes again. Gerald sat on the side of the bed and lifted her up in his arms as he held her until the tears began to roll again. Gerald whispered,

"Mel, I promise you, it is you, it is you I want, and I will be doing as you asked of me last night closing my loose ends to make you fully believe with the words, I just told you and to secure our future together. Are you ready for all that comes with a man like myself? Camera's flashing, red carpet walks, traveling, concerts...and no more working at The Westin."

She responded softly,

"I don't care as long as we are together, I will follow you to moon and back."

Gerald continued to hold her never imagining that he would be having this conversation with Mel, with anyone else for the most part. They sat on the side of the bed with her lying her head on his shoulder and holding hands looking out at the world outside of the windows. What a mess he made in such a short time in Atlanta, but the ending was coming to end of his mess. Today would be the beginning of a fresh start and a new beginning with Mel. He looked down at her and a feeling of relief came over him as he kissed her on her head over and over again until she looked up at him for a kiss. She laid her head back on his shoulder and he told her again,

"Mel, it is you, it's been you the whole time I just kept it to myself in hopes that it would just fade away in fear that you wouldn't want the same thing with me. After my conversation with Nina yesterday I realize that I was the reason that I lost that woman because of my own fears. I am not going to let that happen again and nor am I going to hurt another woman because of my fears. So, if you are really willing to walk with me through this I am here, and you have me forever."

This time the tears rolled down his face and Mel was the one wiping away tears away as she told him,

"Baby, I am here, I have been here since the first time you called me to tell me you needed a room and needed your privacy maintained. I never thought or expected it would go this far. Just promise me that you will not make a fool of me. If you ever feel that this isn't what you want, just talk to me. I beg of you. I don't think I have another hurt from another failed relationship, but I am willing to go with you Gerald Livingston. You know what you have to do to make this happen with us, and I am going to give you time to handle your affairs."

They were both drained as they laid back on the bed in other arms until they fell back asleep again. A few hours went by before a soft knock on the door awakened them followed by the voice of Maria asking if they would be eating it was now three o'clock in the afternoon. Mel responded first with a, "hell yes" because she was starving as she jumped up first and headed to the bathroom to shower with Gerald right behind her. They showered without another steamy sex session and quickly got out and slipped on something to go eat because their stomachs were growling like two unfed grown bears.

They walked out to the breakfast bar greeted Maria and Jay then nothing else was said until you could hear their forks scraping the plates. Jay cleared his throat because it was obvious that they both forgot that he and Maria were there the entire time they made their now late lunch disappear. They all laughed at the same time and Maria spoke with a chuckle,

"You two must have been really starving."

Mel with no hesitation replied with a quick yes while still eating her last forkful as she handed Maria her plate for seconds and the laughter continued as Gerald looked over at her in disbelief with a mouthful of food. After Mel was halfway through her second plate Gerald told her he had to go to Chicago to tie up a few ends, handle some business and check on his condo as well. His mission was to clear everything up both business and personal on his trip to Chicago undecided about keeping his condo and when was he going to ship his vehicles to Atlanta since it looked like he was going to be staying there for good. Gerald offered to take her with him so she could see where he was from, but she reminded him she still had a job and would be there when he returned. He was persistent to get her to come and finally he accepted she wasn't coming so he made transportation arrangements for any travels she may need while he was gone. It was like both of them forgot she even had a car, a car that hadn't moved much since he came into her life. He promised when he returned things would be different and they would continue to grow. Mel asked when he would be leaving and returning with a pouting sad face,

"I will be there for at least a week and you are more than welcome to come up on your off days. I will leave an open plane ticket for you to fly up."

Mel declined again using work as her reason for not going when it was really her fear that this was going to be it for them like the past relationships and at least she would have her job to fall back on as always. No matter how much he tried to convince her to come with him she just kept reverting back to her having to work and promised him she would be there when he returned home to her.

In the midst of his attempt to reassure her that he would be back, and they were heading in a direction to be together, and she needed to start leaving some things at his place, she seemed to pull away. His phone rang and they both got quiet because it was Mia and unlike past times of excusing himself to answer, he answered the call right in front of her and he grabbed her hand as she tried to walk away because she didn't want to hear his phone call like she had done since they had been together. He kept her close while he told Mia that they would have to be strictly business partners from now on because there was someone in his life now that he was going to be seeing on a more serious level. Mel's fight to pull away eased up as she fell on his chest and she listened with tears running down her face. Mia agreed but what he didn't know was that on the other end she was crying because he did what she was actually calling to tell him minus the part there was someone in her life. They went over a few business issues and ended the call as friends and business partners. Mia cried because she really loved Gerald, but she knew from his last visit to her office he was not going to be the man for her, not that she would be able to be totally available because she was still married although separated. Mel asked what about Sandra and if he was sure this was what he really wanted to do. Gerald with no hesitation responded yes this is what he wanted and that he was a little scared because how he was hurt from his last relationship, but he was willing to honestly give them a shot.

The weeks to come they spent every moment together when she wasn't at work. Mel had pretty much had moved into Gerald's place. The Georgia Peaches had been smashed and it was only Mel in his life. In a later conversation also with Mel right by his side he explained the terms of their friendship and professional relationship and Sandra accepted her role as an artist and nothing else.

It was the night before Gerald and Jay would be headed to Chicago for a week. The next morning was hard for them both because it would be the first time they were apart in weeks other than to go to work. They had their normal breakfast before Jay and Gerald left for their flight to Chicago. The ride to drop Mel off for work was spent just laying up on each other as Gerald went through his normal emails and text. They pulled into the garage and Jay met her at the backdoor with Mike, her security detail for the time they would be out of town and she would be picked up to go to and from work by Mr. Sam. Mel did all she could to decline her security detail and Mr. Sam picking her up but nothing she said was convincing as Mike stood patiently waiting for her to go inside for work. Ms. Mel you won't even know I am around so no worries Mam. Gerald smiled and said welcome to the world I asked if you were ready for my love as he blew her a kiss and told her he loved her and he would see her when he returned back home.

The week ahead seemed like it took forever to be over for them both, but the phone calls, text and FaceTime helped them drastically. Gerald's trip to Chicago was successful although he didn't get to see Chris and his family and really needed to stay another week but the time apart from Mel made him homesick nothing like he felt when he would be away from Nina. He put everything in place to have his condo cleaned and his things packed up to be shipped to Atlanta. He scheduled another trip back to Chicago in a few weeks to close out some business and to see Chris and his family as well as Mr. Paul. Mel was so excited that Gerald was coming home but she hadn't been feeling well but never mentioned it to Gerald. So, on her way home she stopped and picked up a pregnancy test it could be a strong possibility that she was pregnant which would explain her exhaustion and a couple of morning sicknesses she had while he was away. Condoms weren't being used at all after the night of their relationship changing conversation. Mike was sworn to secrecy and jokingly he said, I don't know what you are talking about as they both chuckled walking out of the store.

The task now would be how was she going to pull off taking the test without Maria finding out would be the question unless she hurried up and did it in the morning before he came home. She was both anxious and nervous she went straight to the bathroom and took the test. Anxious but scared at the same time she almost dropped it twice. She yelled for Maria to come to the bathroom and there she was sitting on the toilet when Maria walked into the bathroom, Maria nervously asked if she was pregnant and was, she ok as she looked down at the positive sign bleed through strong meaning that is a yes…she is pregnant. Tears of happiness rolled down her face because this has been the best year of her life, she wanted for nothing and a baby would be the biggest blessing that they never disgust. Maria was smiling and crying at the same time as well.

Did Gerald even want kids? He was about to return from Chicago. He was about to release a cd that had been done and sitting just before the breakup with Nina, Sandra's cd was about to be released, the real estate business was growing in leaps and bounds, and they were at the beginning phase of their now official relationship. As usual she had doubts and wondered if this was even a good time for a baby. Maria was full of joy and excitement as she excused herself and finished preparing dinner for Mel and Mike.

Gerald's flight landed early, and he surprised her when he came in the house yelling for Mel like he did everyday full of excitement to see her. She tucked the test away that she slept with on the nightstand and yelled back to him I am coming baby. The hug and kiss were longer than normal then Gerald told her that the condo was being cleaned and packed up then it would be put on the market, he signed another artist to a record deal, his cd was being released in the morning and then he dropped a box in her hand. When she opened the box, it was a set of keys to a car and her mouth dropped as her arms opened wide to hug him,

"Baby it's ok I love you and you deserve it, stop crying"

he told her. As she was about to tell him about her pregnancy test, he pulled her out to the garage and there set a brand-new black Mercedes AMG S-Class.

"When did you do this? How did you get this here? Mike you knew about this?"

The tears of joy rolled down her pretty face and she just jumped into his arms and just hugged him. She could feel the excitement and the smile on his face was a clear sign that he was just as happy as she was, and she didn't want to take the chance and mess up the mood. Gerald convinced her to take him for a ride with Jay and Mike following behind them because of course neither of them could fit in the backseat. They rode around for about an hour before they headed back home to have some lunch. Gerald and Mel spent the night talking about all that happened while he was in Chicago and their future together until he dozed off tired from his flight and now the obvious pre-father signs. Mel curled up under him and tried to figure out how she would tell him he was going to be a father. He woke up long enough to pull her under his arm and she dosed off like she had slept every night, in his arms.

They woke up the next morning to the smell of Maria's cooking and not long into their morning conversation Mel ran to the bathroom with morning sickness. She was sure he heard her so she thought of every excuse she could give him if he asked about it.

"You ok baby? You need anything?"

She told him she must have eaten something that didn't agree with her stomach, but she felt better after she finished throwing up. They brushed their teeth and headed out to eat some breakfast. While they were eating, Gerald was eating everything, and Mel picked over her food as expected.

Gerald asked her if she was ok and suggested they go and lay down for a little while he had a free day once he made a few phone calls and answered some emails. He got a call that he was going to have to fly back to Chicago sooner than he planned which put a frown on Mel face until Gerald told her he would be back home as soon as he is finished and once again, he offered for her to come with him. After the call he phoned Jay to tell him they would be flying out in the morning to go back to Chicago. They laid around the rest of the day and Mel was in pure bliss looking at her soon to be Father to her child. They had dinner with Jay and Mike it was the closest thing to family they all had, and Maria was treated like family as well.

Gerald packed for a few days in Chicago until he saw that Mel was sad again,

"I will finish grabbing a few things in the morning. Let me lay down here with my baby. I promise you once you decide you want to travel with me you will be by my side whenever you want to go baby."

It felt like the minute she closed her eyes it was time to get up and watch him get ready to go to the airport. The alarm sounded and Gerald got up to get ready at four o'clock to be at the airport by five for a seven o'clock departure. She would have to get use to him leaving and returning, this particular time would be harder with the information she was holding inside. He was up and ready to go as she laid in the bed watching him get ready until he said to her,

"Come on baby walk me to the door I have to go."

he grabbed his bag as he stood at the bedroom door waiting for her to get out of the bed noticing she was moving slower than normal. He asked her was she ok and she brushed it off telling him she was just sleepy.

"Get some rest and I will call you when we land in Chicago."

After they kissed and hugged with Jay pulling him out the door, she closed the door and laid against the door. She smiled and dreamed of his face when she would finally tell him. But the magical question still loomed, how do I tell him?

CHAPTER 15

"I Love You and
I Need You"

AFTER TWO DAYS IN CHICAGO Gerald was ready to go back home to Mel. Everywhere he went still had some type of remembrance of Nina. Jay could see it and suggested they visit the Centerfield Lounge after they finished with all the business at hand like old times, he was sure that Mr. Paul would love to see him especially since they didn't get to stop by the last time they were in town. Gerald wanted to go back to their suite but eventually he agreed with some strong persuasion after the last meeting, and they headed to the lounge. As they pulled up in front of the lounge security looked to make sure it was Jay's blacked out Suburban pulling up, it had been over a year since Gerald had been in Centerfield Lounge. Security called into Mr. Paul to let him know Gerald was there and would need a table in the back and immediately he came outside himself to walk him in after he hugged him like a Father who hadn't seen his son in a long time. Jay got out and it was like a family member had returned home when he opened the door for Gerald,

"I love you and you know you are like a son to me. Why would you just shut down and then leave like that son? Come on son I'll have your favorite table ready in few minutes and I have someone you may want to see."

As they entered the lounge some of the regulars saw him it was like a reunion until his table was ready. As he approached his section, he always sat in he saw his best friend Chris. Gerald looked back at Jay realizing he had all of this planned, Jay shrugged his shoulders and smiled. Chris hugged him and behind him was his wife who was like a sister with eyes filled with tears. She hugged him like she didn't want to let him go. Gerald kept telling her,

"I am ok Tammy, I am ok. It is so good to see you two."

Finally, after all the other greetings and welcome backs Gerald took a seat and drank his favorite glass of house wine with an order of his favorite wings catching up with Chris and Tammy. They both tiptoed around the Nina situation not sure if he had addressed it or buried it like so many other situations in the past. There was no need to dodge it he brought it up telling them that it was closed and the good news that he was seeing someone that he was very much happy and in love with.

Tammy of course had fifty questions or so it seemed about the lucky lady and all Gerald said is,

"Her name is Melanie, and she is something special so special that she has even met Jay's approval. She has taken my heart from a place that I vowed to leave it after Nina."

He told them about the conversation he had with Nina he sounded very much at peace with it nothing like over a year ago. Chris gave him a soft pat on the back while telling him that she called asking where he was less than three months after she said I do. Gerald interrupted by telling them he was happy with life again and it was because of Mel. He told them of his three-women escapade which included Mel and she was the one who stole his heart, how she made him want to clean his act up before he got out of control like he was before he met Nina.

"Mel helped to me to see me past my fears of not being like the man I didn't want to be by just being herself and not judging me for my past. She actually reminds me of my Mom. Mel is my happiness she is the reason I was able to come back here and guess what, sell my condo, it sold today. I am having my vehicles shipped to Atlanta and take care of few business deals here in Chicago. Life has been great since I stopped running from her chasing one woman I knew wasn't going anywhere because she is married but separated and the other is an artist that I have signed. You may remember her we did a song or two together, Sandra. I know I am talking a lot but let me apologize for leaving the way I did, I almost completely snapped after Nina left me. I sat for a year in my condo and it looked like it too. If that was the pain my mom felt when my sperm donor left, her and I and made her look like a fool I truly, truly understand how she felt."

He paused after that last comment and sipped on his wine. Chris and Tammy both knew that was a touchy situation especially since his mother never bounced back from the hurt, she just endured it and put her all into

Gerald. She worked tirelessly to see that he had all he needed, wanted and that his education was top notch. Before he could say anything, else Mr. Paul silenced the bar for a toast to his son, Gerald,

"I have known this young man since he was a teenager begging for a job to sweep floors and put the trash out. A few days a week I let him work until I found out his mother had no clue what he was doing, and he was supposed to be in tutoring classes. (The entire bar laughed) He was mad at me when I told him to go home and he told me when I become famous, you'll want me here then. Well guess who came back with his three-piece band as the G Band, my son. Now look at him he is world known and bounced back from the loss of his mother as well as whatever else has been handed to him. I pray that your move to Atlanta brings you all the happiness you have earned and deserve. Always remember this is home! Raise your glasses to my son Gerald Livingston to many of you and G to me!"

The bar roared

"Cheers!"

Filled with emotion which showed all over his face he tried to offer a response but could only utter,

"Thank you, Mr. Paul and my Centerfield Lounge family I will be back to visit. This will always be home to me no matter where I go."

After all of the chatter calmed down and the folks stopped coming over to the table to wish him well Chris, Tammy and Gerald resumed their reunion and farewell. Chris once again inquired for more information about this new love and when they would be meeting her. Gerald anxiously spoke more about Mel from the day they connected on a personal level after his return to Atlanta and how she stuck by him through his foolishness with the other women. He shared that it was Mia that helped him to see that covering the hurt with all the women he only added to his already mess of a life. It was the last in-depth conversation with Mia that made him look at his part that he played in the decision for Nina to leave the way that she did. He didn't totally agree with how she left still but he finally understood and accepted his part that he played in her decision to leave. He also shared with them that she wasn't happy nor safe in her marriage and he felt bad about it but in a saving grace way that he offered her his place if she decided to leave her husband and needed a place to stay.

Tammy sat in an attentive but total silence stance while listening to every word just like the overprotective sister she could be that he never had. Gerald's phone vibrated and judging by the big smile on his face it was no secret it was the mystery lady, Mel. The text was one of her normal I love you and I miss you, but she added I can't wait until you get home on Sunday. Smiling the whole time, he responded to her text and seeing him happy made Tammy and Chris happy as well.

"How much longer are you here G?"

Chris asked while he continued to text Mel.

"I am supposed to be here for a week, and I must admit I am ready to go back home to Mel at the first free moment I can. Excuse me for a minute I need to make a call."

Mel laid on the bed smiling looking at Gerald's picture on her phone until it rang reflecting the Dr office number, she had been feeling a little more ill after the pregnancy test. Tears began to roll down her face as the nurse was about to tell her,

"Melanie you are..."

then the line clicked with a call from Gerald,

"Please hold on?" Don't hang up please this is an important call, but I promise you I will be fast"

as she switched lines.

"Are you ok, Gerald?"

he replied,

"Yes, I am ok baby, just slipped away so I could hear your voice. I really miss you. This is the second time I have been away from you since we have officially been together, and I don't like it. Are you ok baby? You need anything?"

Mel was so excited to hear his voice she almost forgot about the call on the other line, so she quickly responded she was ok, about to eat and lay back down to watch some tv. Telling him to go back to his friends and text her. They ended the call as they always did with,

"I promise to love you more"

then she switched back over to the nurse who informed her,

"Ms. Santiago you're expecting, and the Dr wants to see you in a week. I have an appointment for four o'clock on Tuesday?"

Mel with tears of joy confirmed and ended the call. Laying there with tears of happiness and joy she wondered how she would tell him. Maria walked in to bring her some dinner and saw the tears figuring it was because she was missing Mr. Gerald until Mel said,

"Maria... (then she paused) I am really pregnant"

Maria smiled and said,

"I knew you were by the way you have been eating, sleeping and when I cleaned the bathroom you left another pregnancy test stick and box in the trashcan."

Mel asked,

"How do I tell him? Maria I am so happy"

Maria responded,

"Wait until he gets home but from now on you have to eat, you're eating for two Ms. Mel." as she smiled and walked out of the room.

Gerald made his way back to the table and after another glass of wine and some more chicken wings he let Chris and Tammy know that he would be back with Mel if they didn't make it to Atlanta before. He attempted to pay the tab, but Mr. Paul refused his money he let Jay know he was ready to go back to his suite. Jay followed behind him as he walked around and began to say his farewells to everybody. Chris hugged him telling him he was happy for him and hoped that he would come back to visit with the new lady soon. Gerald gave him a look like it was a no brainer that he would be back with Mel then he hugged Chris as he grabbed for Tammy who was now teary eyed for a group hug at the end of the bar. Almost like a sweet and sour piece of candy things went from sweet to sour when Jay leaned over to let Gerald know that Nina and her sister walked in and Nina was asking for him. Gerald smiled and responded,

"Tell them to come over here I have a few minutes to spare"

Tammy's face read of disgust, but Gerald reassured her he was fine and to calm down. Security walked up with Nina and her sister and Gerald greeted them both with a hug and asked if they were ok. He also signaled for Mr. Paul to take care of them for the night and he would cover their tab. Jay slipped Mr. Paul some cash and nudged Gerald to let him know it was time to go. Gerald said,

"Ladies enjoy your evening I am headed out, Nina it is good to see you and Michelle it was a pleasure to see you again as well. Nina don't forget if you need anything please don't hesitate to give me a call. I mean it."

Nina thanked him and let him know she was good, and it was good to see him as well. Jay gave her a hug before he walked Gerald, Tammy and Chris to the door.

Tammy asked him,

"What the hell was that Gerald Livingston? You are really ok and have moved on. I am so happy for you and now I really need to meet this Mel."

Gerald grabbed her hand and pulled her to keep walking as he smiled with a feeling of relief that it was over, and he was ok with it. Nina walked away while looking back at Gerald. Mr. Paul had one of the servers take Nina and her sister to a table so he could say goodbye to his son. Jay and the lounge security walked them outside to the blacked-out Suburban that was waiting at the curb for Gerald with the door open and they all did a final farewell. Tammy was the one who didn't want to let go but Chris took care of her as she stood there now in tears that Gerald was leaving them and not sure when he would be back. Once they were in the truck before Jay could say a word Gerald said,

"I am ready to go home, to my new home and my lady. I needed to see Nina again and I know for sure I am done, and I am ok with it."

Jay instructed the driver to take them back to the hotel and as they pulled off Jay just tapped Gerald on his knee with his huge hand that covered his entire knee. It was a quiet ride and with the normal garage entrance they went up to the adjoining room suite where they talked for hours until they both fell asleep. Like clockwork at six a.m. Mel's text him woke him up with a smile and really made him want to head back home that much more.

Gerald ordered room service and looked over some paperwork, made sure his cars would be shipped and the closing on his condo was still for Friday. He got online to see if the flights could be bumped up because he was really ready to go home. Once he confirmed the flight Jay was finally able to convince him to go down to the gym with him for a workout to kill some time. After about an hour of cardio and finishing on the weights Jay asked,

"Are you ok? Are you really over her now?"

and Gerald replied,

"I am done I am ok Brother, seriously. I am just sorry that it had to end the way it did, honestly if I hadn't been the man that I was it wouldn't have ended at all. But I am in a good place and all the broken pieces are coming together."

as he sat up off of the weight bench. Jay could hear it in his voice that Gerald was done. Relieved and happy at the same time he said,

"Ms. Mel is good for you. I like her and I hope that it all works out. Now come on Brother let's get you back home to Ms. Mel."

One last text to Mel before he showered and began his day,

"I love you so much and I miss you and I need you. I am cutting this trip short baby I can't do too much longer away from you. I will be coming home tomorrow."

CHAPTER 16

"Coming Home"

AFTER ONLY THREE DAYS IN Chicago a place he called home and vowed never to leave, Gerald was ready to leave. He looked out the suite window looking over the city remembering his childhood to adulthood to his traveling in and out of it and now he was ready to go back to his new place he now called home in Atlanta. Reminiscing about running down the street to meet his mom at the bus stop, walking home with Jay and Chris from school, Jay teased him about being a musician and singer but who did Gerald call for his security when his football career ended suddenly in college, Jay. The three of them were inseparable and no matter where life took Gerald, he was still "G" to them. Gerald's mom took Jay as her own son when he was ready to give up on everything. So many memories ran through his mind and even the years he spent in love with Nina, hopelessly in love. The plans for this time in his life was supposed to be with Nina, but because of his way of dealing with the hurt from his Father was not to deal with it he lost Nina. He was able to accept that they were in two different places in life now and he could honestly say he wanted the best for Nina, and it wasn't him. That portion of the memories about he and Nina brought tears to his eyes. Jay walked over and placed one of those big hands on his shoulder to tell him,

"The car will be here in twenty minutes we will ride pass the old neighborhood before we head to the airport. I will let you get yourself together while I get our bags together. We are headed home brother, to a place of new life and your new lady."

Gerald got himself together slipped his sport jacket on, baseball cap and sent a text to Mel he would be home tonight and couldn't wait to see her. Instantly she responded I love you and I miss you too. Jay walked in with the bellhop,

"G the truck is here"

Jay said and, on the way, to home they were heading. The blacked out Suburban that Gerald brought Jay for his personal use, but Jay insisted it be used for Gerald's transportation when they rode around Chicago, rode slowly down all the familiar Chicago streets until it turned into the old neighborhood so Gerald could see the old neighborhood and his old house that he brought and fixed up but never lived in it again. Everything was updated accept the furniture that his Mom left.

"Jay how much time do we have? I need to make a stop."

Gerald suddenly asked Jay, Jay was puzzled as he looked down at his watch,

"Two hours or so. Why?"

instantly Gerald ordered the driver,

"Take me to Pentecost Street sir, Brown and Sons Jewelers."

Jay had no idea what he was about to do. Gerald just continued to look out the window at the now busy traffic until they pulled up in front of the jewelry store and Gerald was out of the truck and walking into the store before Jay or the driver were out to open his door.

"Gerald"

Mr. Brown exclaimed with a big smile,

"What are you doing here without a phone call first or some kind of warning, Jay?"

as he stopped and looked at Jay. Gerald went straight to the women's rings showcases and found a wedding band an Astor by Blue Nile five carat diamond wedding and engagement ring set,

"I want them both and can they be sized to fit a size six right now?"

Always ready to do whatever Gerald asked of him Mr. Brown pulled out the twenty-five-thousand-dollar piece ready to work a deal but, Gerald didn't hear a word he said as he instantly pulled out his credit card.

"I'll take them now. They look better out of the case. I need it to be a size six. I am pressed for time and I am paying whatever the sticker says Mr. Brown."

Jay knew now that Mel was definitely who was going to be the woman in Gerald's life. All he could do was smile and pat Gerald on the back. Mel text him about ten times by now, but Gerald stood in the front window as he looked up at the sky he whispered to his mom,

"Mommy, I know I have made a mess in Atlanta, but I am about to fix it and seal the deal this time. I pray that you will be happy for me because I am happy."

Jay walked up behind him and said,

"She is happy Brother; you have been a success with no drama or bad news. No kids out of wedlock. You've finally dealt with your fear and look at the reward it got you, peace and Ms. Mel."

Gerald just turned around and shook Jay hand and told him,

"Jay, thank you for always having my back, I really appreciate you and love you like a Brother. Jay, I love Mel, I really love her, and I am in love with her. She saved my sinking heart and has taken care of it very carefully. I thought love would never happen again after Nina, but Mel is every part of my happiness now. I am not going to lose this one because of my painful past."

Jay was floored and just gave the ok and hugged Gerald. Mr. Brown came from the back with the rings boxed, bagged and ready to go thanking Gerald for his purchase, time was nearing there check in, so they rushed to the front door as he handed Mr. Brown a handful of cash as Gerald promised to come back and see him the next time he was in town and not in such a rush to catch a flight. He extended his apology as Jay lightly pushed him out the door and Mr. Brown told him it was good to see him. They were back in the truck and headed to the airport Gerald continued to look out the window he was ready to board the plane headed to Atlanta now even more ready get back home to Mel.

O'Hare International Airport two miles ahead the signs read as Gerald's smile became even bigger. Meanwhile Mel was home trying to figure out how she was going to tell him she was expecting his first child. Maria had given her a few ideas, but nothing seemed to be good enough or the perfect way to do it and now he was hours away from returning home. Like some type of dignitary, the airport security and staff whisked them through the airport to their plane. Mel's heart began to race, and the questions followed. How do I tell him? When do I tell him?

Gerald was in his seat now and of course with his headphones on and a playlist long enough to last the duration of the flight. Jay on alert as usual until Gerald tapped him on the leg and said,

"Relax Jay I am ok, we are ok, just relax."

Jay's massive chest relaxed for a half of second or so it seemed until Gerald laid his seat back and closed his eyes.

Flashbacks continued of his mom and all she sacrificed for him. She never dated after his father broke her heart. They had a mother son relationship that was unbreakable, and he made sure the world knew it. The night he won his first Grammy she passed away right after they announced his name. Ms. Mona loved Gerald with all she had, and he loved her the same. There were qualities in Mel that resembled his mother her soft and gentle spirit, the way she loved him and supported him, but she had a fiery side as well that demanded the best from him and for him, she comforted him and more importantly she had a love for him that although it hadn't been that long it felt like a lifetime with her it could only get stronger from this point.

Back at home Mel laid in the bed and rubbed her belly with a smile on her face. She finally had a man that not only loved her physically but in every aspect of her mere existence. Tenderly he handled her and took care of her, she wanted for nothing and melted with his every touch and word. Their small disagreements which she could count on one hand only lasted for what seemed to be minutes but the making up lasted for days. His mom always told him one day you will be a good man to a woman who will love you like you need to be loved just before she got really sick. Making him promise never to do another woman like his father hurt her and no kids until marriage. Life finally made sense and Mel completed it for him. What could have turned into a fiasco of many women ongoing till it exploded causing his mother to turn over in her grave, Mia saved him from helping him to see that Mel was the one for him. He knew in his heart that his mother was looking down now on him in complete approval of his decision.

The stewardess came over the intercom to alert that they would be landing in about ten minutes and to please prepare for landing. As they put their seatbelts on Gerald looked over at Jay and said,

"Well buddy life will change forever when we get home, home to my soon to be wife. If she says yes."

as the plane began its touch down Gerald said a prayer. Jay held his hand as they prayed together. The plane landed in Atlanta and Jay and Gerald were escorted off the plane to Mr. Sam who greeted them with a smile.

"Mr. G, Jay how was your trip? Glad to have you back in Atlanta. I will have you home shortly permitting the traffic" as he closed the door and made sure their luggage was in the trunk. As the shiny black dark tinted Lincoln limo pulled away from the curb into the busy airport traffic Gerald text Mel to let her know he would be home soon. Instantly she responded, at the hair salon I will be home in about an hour and I love you. Jay questioned, how would he ask her and was he ready to ask her? Gerald just stirred out the window and said,

"Jay, I am going propose to her as soon as I see her, I will make sure she knows I never want to be without her and damn sure don't ever want to lose her. I feel so good about this and her. I have been on the table with everything and honestly, I don't want to be with anyone else ever again. Mel has truly made me forget about the idea of never loving again. Every one of them women I slept with or engaged with in some type of way couldn't add up to what she brings to the table and sure couldn't move me like she has and does. I loved Nina with all I had, and I would have married her but my experience from my childhood scared me and minus a child she repeated the history of my father as a result of my failure to deal with my own past hurt that I allowed myself to live in fear of hurting someone I loved like my father who broke my mother's heart. Seeing that hurt that my mother thought she was hiding from me made me feel like I was meant to take care of her forever and I did until the day she passed away. I then unknowingly and selfishly poured my hurt into Nina until she left me, and I felt like my mother left me all over again. Then I gave up on life, work, love and myself. Mel has taught me how to love and love what I am doing again. I can't tell you how dark my life was when Nina left, even when the sun shined in the windows, the Grammy's, hit after hit even after my Mom passed nothing really made me happy nor did it take away the pain. But when I came to Atlanta Mel was the first woman to extend that genuine love and nurturing and I almost missed it in the midst of my foolishness running with Mia and Sandra she never asked for a dime but gave me everything I shouldn't have had until now. She has truly stolen and repairing my broken heart and helps to put it back together every day filling it with her love"

Jay was lost for words because he never told him any of this and he finally responded,

"G, I am with you, always been with you and anything you need from me you know it is nothing but a request away. I will have Mike to take over as her permanent security if that is suitable for you and her. I will take care of it in the morning."

Gerald was in agreement as he continued to look out the window.

As they approached the building in the middle of the block on Peachtree in Buckhead never looked so pretty after leaving Chicago. Gerald cracked the window to inhale the fresh Georgia air, home at last he thought as the car stopped in front of the building and for the first time there was no crowd or pictures being taken which made for a peaceful return home. For the first time Mr. Sam was asked to come upstairs for a few minutes, he was shocked as he made a U-turn to pull into the garage and parked on Gerald's level double parked behind the spaces marked for the Penthouse. Jay met Mr. Sam in the hallway and as they entered the penthouse his eyes lit up like it was the Rockefeller Plaza Christmas tree on Christmas day. Gerald pointed over to the living room area,

"Have a seat Mr. Sam I have something for you"

Jay looking lost because Gerald was full of surprises today. Gerald came back with an envelope full of cash thanking Mr. Sam for his services from the day he landed in Atlanta and requested that he will continue to serve Mel and himself with his transportation services, exclusively now. Lost for words Mr. Sam said,

"Yes, of course Mr. Gerald. Thank you for the opportunity."

Gerald shook his hand and hugged him while telling Jay,

Get with Mr. Sam and get the contracts and all of his information so that he will be able to travel everywhere with us when needed."

Gerald turned to Maria and handed her an envelope filled with cash and asked if she would be the fulltime cook and housekeeper. Tear filled and with no hesitation she accepted his request and hugged him. As Maria was letting go Mel walked in from the salon pushing Mike to the side as she ran to Gerald whose arms were open wide to catch her. They hugged and kissed for what seemed forever until Jay cleared his throat reminding them others were in the room. Coming up for air they looked around the room and Mel greeted everyone with a big smile on her beautiful face not letting go of Gerald. Small talk began about their trip to Chicago and happy they were back home then Gerald called for everyone's attention, Jay knew what was about to happen as he whispered in Gerald's ear,

"Are you serious? Again G? What else could you possibly have to give or say?"

Tears filled his eyes, and he was choked up as he spoke looking around at all of them before he directed his attention to Mel,

"This room is filled with people who have been through one of my lowest points in my life. You each have played a part in who I have been resurrected back to, today. I will forever be indebted to you all, each and every one of you. Jay, my cousin, my brother, my friend and my protector who has been there from the start and traveled from one end of the world to the other and back. Maria you came in and took care of my needs, cleaned my home, cooked for me and at times made me eat when I didn't want to. Mr. Sam, Mr. Sam you were the first person who I met when I got off the bus, shared words of wisdom and have been providing me with the best transportation services"

Then he paused…

"Melanie Santiago you remember when I called you for a room when I got here, and you took care of me from day one. (The tears flowed down his face) you have been my everything and foolishly I almost lost you, not that I was trying to lose you. You have given me your love, friendship, heart and you have given me life again and I probably could never repay you. But if you allow me to and you will have me to, I will give you the rest of my lifetime trying."

As he got down on one knee and pulled out the ring and she burst out crying yelling repeatedly,

"Yes Gerald, Yes! Yes!"

Finally, she gave him her hand to slip the ring on as he asked,

"Melanie Santiago will you marry me?"

Mel cried and again she cried out,

"Yes Gerald, Yes Gerald, Yes!"

He picked her up and held her until they both stopped crying.

Mel asked for a moment to thank everyone for accepting her especially Jay, whom she said she thought was so mean in the beginning but realized he was just doing his job and cares for Gerald in a way not even she could. She stepped away from Gerald while still holding his hands as she said,

"The man of the hour and my now soon to be husband, you think I gave life back to you, no baby you have given me a life to share with you and another one between us"

as she began to rub her stomach.

Al Johnson

Gerald pulled her in tight,

"Mel…are you serious, you are…you're pregnant?"

He picked her up and held her as the tears flowed from them both, her tears were because she was so happy that he was excited for the surprise of her being pregnant and he had proposed to her, Gerald's because his mother wasn't there to see him so happy, but the tears were also for the happiness he felt at that very moment. The room was filled with so much happiness and everyone hugged Mel, rubbed her stomach and took a look at the beautiful ring Gerald had put on her finger. Happiness for them both filled the room and they repeatedly congratulated them both until Gerald cleared his throat enough to say,

"All things come in time family, friends, love and companionship…In Due Time"

Printed in the United States
by Baker & Taylor Publisher Services